CORPORATE
INVASION

TERESITA E. DZIADURA

CORPORATE
INVASION

TERESITA E. DZIADURA

Published in Canada by Engen Books, St. John's, NL.

Library and Archives Canada Cataloguing in Publication

Title: Corporate invasion / Teresita E. Dziadura.
Names: Dziadura, Teresita E., author.
Identifiers: Canadiana (print) 20210213922 | Canadiana (ebook) 20210214066 |
ISBN 9781774780442
  (softcover) | ISBN 9781774780435 (PDF)
Classification: LCC PS8607.Z53 C67 2021 | DDC C813/.6—dc23

Distributed by:
Engen Books
www.engenbooks.com
submissions@engenbooks.com

First mass market paperback printing: May 2021

Cover Design: Ellen Curtis
Cover Image: Shutterstock

This book is dedicated to my incredible niece, Courtney Downey.

Your light, strength and courage will always inspire us. Your spirit lives on in the people you touched.

You are missed.

CHAPTER ONE

A stillness had enveloped Boston in these early hours as Jason made his way to the bus stop. Heavy, rain-filled clouds hung low, muting the sounds of the people just starting their day.

Once it had been a pleasant walk with a cool spring breeze, the city stirring to life, and the birds singing in the trees. Now, no birdsong greeted him while he ran beneath the green canopy. They were all hiding from the incessant rain. Everything felt heavy and oppressive as he darted into the protection of the shelter.

"Frigging soaked again," Jason thought as he huddled in the corner, shaking the water from his arms and trying to avoid the ever-growing puddle. It had been a full week of steady thundershowers and he hadn't seen the sun in weeks. It felt as if day had turned into night. Streetlights stayed on during the day, briefly dimming each time lightening arched across the sky.

In addition to the unceasing rain, it was hot like July in Louisiana than April in Massachusetts. The temperatures had started creeping up since the first of the month. The unseasonal weather was so humid that some of the runners had gotten sick and passed out during the already gruelling Boston Marathon. One guy had died of heat stroke.

On the news the night before, Jason had watched as meteorologists expressed their bafflement by the never-ending rain and heat that seemed to be focused solely on the Boston area. The clouds seemed to be hovering over the city in defiance of jet stream and other weather patterns.

It wasn't even 7 am and it was already in the nineties. Boston had become a sauna that was threatening to become a swamp. There were announcements for rivers that were inching towards overflowing their banks and sandbags were being offered for areas that were at risk for flooding.

Jason glared at the puddle as it made its approach. The puddle grew bigger with each raindrop that fell until it had him cornered in the dilapidated bus shelter which always smelled faintly of old pee. With the heat and dampness, it had begun to smell more like standing inside a urinal and the stench made him gag. His attention wavered as he heard the low drone of his bus speeding down the street. He watched it approach, late as usual, pass his stop and keep on going. He leapt the puddle and almost cleared it. Tepid water splashed up around his legs and soaked his Converse shoes as he ran through the downpour yelling and waving, hoping the driver saw him. With a screech of hydraulic brakes, the bus stopped and the doors opened, but not before Jason was dripping wet. He jumped on, swiped his bus pass and nodded to Ralph, the regular driver, as he headed to the back.

"Gonna be another great day," Jason grumbled to himself as he folded his lanky body into one of the seats. He poked his earbuds into his ears, cranked up his music, laid his backpack on his lap, and closed his eyes as pools of water formed at his feet. His dark auburn hair hung limp over his face. Jason's normal complexion was pale but today he was flushed with his short run in the heat, and it made the light freckles on his face stand out.

"What utter shit this is."

"You got that right, mac," a raspy voice said.

Jason opened his eyes to see an odd-looking man staring back at him. Greying black hair in a tangle of unkempt dreads, over a round weathered face. Cool grey eyes peered out from below a pair of bushy eyebrows. A long scraggly beard covered a tie-dyed shirt stained with who knows what, which was tucked into a pair of well-worn camo pants. A backpack sat on the seat next to the man.

"Beg your pardon?" Jason inquired, pulling the earbuds out.

"I concur with your assessment that this is utter shit."

"I'm sorry, I didn't realize I'd said that out loud."

"It *is* a Monday after all." The man smiled, showing off teeth that would give an orthodontist nightmares. "What's got a young fella like yourself in such a slump?"

Jason swallowed hard and tried not to stare. It was a well-known, unspoken rule of those who ride the bus: don't talk to strangers. You keep to yourself, hunker down and hope to go unnoticed. Jason had broken that rule, twice now, and he was trapped. "Ummm..."

The older man just sat there, looking at Jason. Waiting for a reply.

"I don't like to complain…" Jason continued. "But… do you catch this bus very often?"

"I'm on it with you nearly every morning."

"Oh. Sorry. I never noticed."

The man just laughed. "No offence taken. You fly onto the bus, listening to your music, and hop off in the warehouse district."

Jason felt a little creeped out by this but nodded. "Yeah, that's my morning routine. But doesn't it piss you off how it's always late?"

"I suppose it might if I had someplace to be to. I don't."

"Oh," Jason said.

The man shrugged. "It's better than sittin' out in the rain all day."

"Why'd you do tha—" Jason cut himself off as he looked from the backpack to the man and back again.

"Yes sir, hobo extraordinaire," the man said with a nod and a smile. "Name's Frank, by the way."

"Jason. Pleased to meet you."

"Likewise, but you haven't told me why this Monday is so shitty. Ralph's always late. That's nothin' new."

"Keep it up, Frank, and you can go back to walkin'," Ralph called out.

"I'm sorry, Ralph. I'm the one complaining," Jason rushed to his new friend's defence.

"Don't worry, Ralph's not gonna kick me off. No one else will talk to him so he's stuck with me."

Ralph's reply was a simple disgruntled snort.

"So, other than Ralph's lack of punctuality, what's got you down?"

He looked at Frank, homeless but still upbeat and happy. Jason had been so upset over things like missing breakfast and sleeping in; when comparing his lot with that of Frank's, he felt silly.

He smiled and said, "You know what? Not as much as I thought."

"That's a good outlook to have, young fella."

Jason kept his fears of losing his job to himself. A frown slipped over his face as he thought of having to face his weasel of a boss. He'd already been warned twice. He'd been made well aware that management didn't give a damn about Jason's *excuses* regarding his transportation woes. Last time he was written up he'd been told, "That sounds like a you problem. If you need to, catch an earlier bus." Which would be perfect except this was the earliest bus.

How'd he ever gotten to this point? Frank stood and moved up to a seat near Ralph as Jason fell silent and adopted a far-away look.

It was heading towards midnight on a Friday. The bar where Jason worked was crowded with all the regulars; an interesting mix of leather-clad middle-aged bikers and leopard-print-wearing cougars. Tonight, there were a couple of new bodies that had shown up. They didn't seem to mind that the place smelled of stale beer and reeked of loneliness.

Jason looked around at his handiwork. He'd spent all afternoon preparing for tomorrow night's Fourth of July party and barbeque. Banners hung from the ceiling, a large flag decorated one wall, and the candles cast little star patterns onto the tables from the red, white, and blue holders.

"It's gonna have to do," he said with a shrug. He just hoped they lasted out the night.

Jason began humming along to Willie Nelson's "Help Me Make It Through the Night" playing on the jukebox as he turned back to cleaning glasses and topping off the bowls of nuts.

"That's my theme song," Jason thought.

He was dead tired. He hadn't slept in over twenty-four hours after working the night before, classes all afternoon and then back to work tonight. He gave the bottles of whiskey that lined the shelves a quick wistful look. All he wanted to do was lay down in bed with a drink, some take-out, and Netflix for just one night. "After finals," he kept promising himself.

"Help Me Make It Through the Night" had finished and "Blue Eyes Crying in the Rain" came on.

"Jesus, Duke? Don't you listen to anyone but Willie?" Jason didn't hate country, but he was to the point that he probably knew more of the words to Willie's, Waylon's, and Johnny's songs than they did.

"Ain't nobody but Willie," Duke said as he racked up another set on the pool table for him and his husband, Bear. Duke and Bear were a couple of regulars and the unofficial bouncers for Wanderer's Roadhouse. They were big men with long shaggy beards, and they lived in leather and denim. They were the owner's best friends and Jason had standing orders that the couple could drink and eat for free, but they never did.

Jason started singing along with Willie, "In the twilight glow I see her, blue eyes cryin' in the rain. When we kissed goodbye and parted, I knew we'd never meet again."

As he sang, he moved to the far end near a small sink and counter to cut up limes. The pair he called the Tequila Sisters had arrived and they'd soon be looking for their line-up of shots.

He had his back to the crowd but with Duke and Bear on guard he had no concerns.

He didn't even so much as look up when he heard the door open, not until all the normal sounds of clinking pool balls and chatter stopped. "What the fuck?" he thought as he looked in the cracked mirror that was behind the bar but gave a full view of the floor.

Jason's mouth went dry and everything went sideways. She was the most beautiful woman he'd ever seen. Every eye in the place turned to follow her as she made her way to near where Jason worked and slipped onto a stool. It wasn't just her looks; it was her presence. Jason figured she couldn't be more than five feet tall, but she carried herself like a six-foot queen. She owned the space she occupied.

More than one biker licked his lips as he stared at her. She was either a master at ignoring the unwanted attention or was oblivious to the leering she'd garnered from the patrons. A starving man wouldn't have looked at a steak as hungrily as these guys were looking at her. Even Duke and Bear were staring.

Jason dropped his paring knife into the sink and turned to serve her, hoping he wasn't gawping when she leaned against the bar. His mouth went dry when he tried to speak.

"Hey," Jason said.

She looked up at him inquiringly. Her bright blue eyes made his heart skip a beat, but he hid his interest behind his bartender persona. "What can I getcha?"

"Whiskey, neat. Please."

"Any particular one?"

"Whatever your top shelf is."

Jason laughed. "Here, that would be Jim Beam."

Her nose scrunched with distaste.

"Hmm. Bourbon." She hesitated. "Any Scotch?"

Jason shook his head. "No ma'am. Just straight American bourbon."

"That will be fine but add a little ice to it," she said with a sigh.

"You got it."

A small smile pulled at the corners of her mouth as she accepted the drink. "Thanks."

Jason stood there, feeling awkward, as she looked down in to the amber liquid, swirling it in her glass. Small waves of the bourbon splashed over the ice. She took a sip and closed her eyes, savouring it. "Not too bad," Jason heard her whisper to the glass.

He gave himself a shake and stepped to the side a little and picked up one of the glasses to give it a polish. He was still close enough for conversation if she wanted to talk but far enough to not be creepy. While he worked, he continued watching her from the corner of his eye. The soft lights cast her face in a gentle shadow. She was far out of the league of every guy and girl in this bar, himself included.

Jason desperately wanted to talk to her and hoped she would start a conversation. She looked like she was worried about something and his job was ten percent tending bar and ninety percent therapist, but she remained silent. It wasn't normal for him to feel this awkward around women, but the words didn't want to come. He just stood there, polishing that same glass over and over. He was so focused on her that he hadn't even noticed the background noise returning or the jukebox switching to ZZ Top's "Legs."

"Jase," a biker sporting a thick black beard yelled from the other end, making Jason almost drop the glass. "Stop staring at *her tits and give me a god damned beer."*

Everyone laughed and Jason flushed bright pink as the woman looked up at him, raising her perfectly sculpted eyebrow. Looking back and forth between the biker and the woman, he stammered, "I wasn't... I mean I'd never... I mean... Oh fuck it." Angrily he poured a beer and shoved the glass at the laughing biker. Beer slopped over the rim and the biker tossed a five-dollar bill at Jason.

"Fuck off, Jack," Jason said as he grabbed the rag and started scrubbing the bar top, focusing on anything except for her.

Jack laughed all the harder as he re-joined his friends.

His humiliation complete, Jason prayed she'd just leave. He didn't see the small smile crease the corners of her lips as she began to watch him.

***

"Another whiskey. Please?" said a soft melodic voice.

Jason had been scrubbing the same spot on the opposite end of the bar from her and hadn't noticed her moving. His heart stopped. It was her. His face flushed all over again.

"Sure."

He poured the drink and served it without once making eye contact. As he placed the fresh glass in front of her she said, "My name's Amanda."

"Jason." His voice cracked and it came out more of a croak.

She grinned and his face turned pink for the third time that night, but as their eyes met, time stood still.

"Hey baby," a rough voice broke the connection and the two of them looked away, embarrassed.

Amanda turned and found a middle-aged man sitting next to her. He was an unfortunate looking thing with mousy brown

hair that was thinning on top and just a little grey at the tem-
ples. His gaunt face was sallow and sported two days worth of
stubble. He was wearing a rumpled dress shirt with his begin-
ner's beer gut hanging over the tops of his jeans. As he talked, he
twisted his wedding ring around on his finger.

"Can I help you?" Amanda asked.

"My name is Colin. I'm one of Jase's regulars and I just
wanted to ask you a question. Do you drink milk?"

Amanda looked at Jason, who was glaring at the man.

"Yeah, I know you. If it were up to me, you'd never set foot
in this place again." Jason thought as he recognized the guy
and had no use for him. Colin was married. He was a complete
a leech who had trouble understanding the word no from the
women he hit on every night.

"Does your wife know you're here?" Jason asked.

Colin glared at Jason. "Angie is staying with her mother.
Now fuck off and leave me and this lovely lady to talk."

Colin looked Amanda up and down, stopping to stare down
her blouse.

He didn't seem to understand personal space, but Amanda
was not easily intimidated.

"To answer your question, no, I don't drink milk. Why
would you ask a complete stranger such an odd question?"

Colin frowned. "You were supposed to say 'yes.'"

"Why? I don't like milk."

"Because then I'd say, 'Because it sure did your body
good.'"

"Oh." Amanda paused with her head tipped to one side. She
was looking at Colin with a perplexed expression. "What a bi-
zarre thing to say."

Amanda spun her stool, turning her back to Colin and fac-

ing the bar top once again. She had just picked up her drink when a hand grabbed her wrist, making her drop her glass. It smashed on the floor beneath her feet. Scowling, she looked from the glass to the hand that was still holding her arm and up into the man's face.

"Let go of me."

"I just wanted to talk to you."

"I do not want to talk to you. You are weird and old." Amanda sniffed and wrinkled her nose in disgust. "And you smell like a dead skunk."

"You bitch," Colin snarled, his face screwing up in anger. Amanda's hands were in white-knuckled fists as she faced Colin, chin up and unafraid.

Colin stared at her in shock.

"I said, let go of my wrist," she said coldly.

Colin's bluster faded quickly, and his hand slipped from her wrist.

Jason moved to stand between Amanda and Colin, forcing the other man to step back. "Colin, I think it's time you went home."

"You can't tell me what to do."

"I can and I am. You're cut off. Now go home."

Duke and Bear had appeared beside.

Jason. Duke reached for Colin while Bear stood there with his arms crossed over his chest.

"Jason's right. You've had more than enough to drink tonight," Duke said, taking him by the back of the shirt, all but lifting him from the ground. His feet tapped the ground as he tried to stand on his own as Duke escorted him to the doors.

"We'll have a chat with the owner about your continued patronage," Bear said as they chucked the man out the door and

tossed his jacket and briefcase behind him.

    Duke snorted disgustedly.

    "Accountants."

    "Sorry about that," Jason said as he started cleaning up the broken glass.

    "It's not your fault. I'm learning it comes with the territory of being female."

    There was silence while he finished sweeping and mopping. He stepped behind the bar and said: "I'll get you a fresh bourbon. A double, on the house."

    "Thanks." Amanda accepted the drink and took a sip. "What time are you off?"

    "Huh?" Jason was caught completely off guard.

    She smiled even wider. "What time do you finish work?"

    "Umm, when we close. Two am."

    "I think I'll hang around until then. If that's okay with you?"

    "Sure?" he said.

    "Thanks. We can grab a coffee and maybe a bite to eat once you're done."

    Jason was flummoxed. "Kay," was all he said.

    She didn't say another word to him until Jason announced last call and Jack yelled back, "Hurry up, boys, and drink 'em down. Jase wants to get laid tonight."

    Jason flushed again while Amanda looked confused. Their reactions made the crowd laugh all the harder.

CHAPTER TWO

Dinner ended up being burgers and fries from Del's Diner, a twenty-four-hour greasy spoon not far from Jason's apartment. It was small, and while it wasn't in an old rail car, the diner looked like it had stepped straight out of a 1950's sitcom, long and narrow with booths along one window-lined wall, complete with black and white tiled floor. Worn dark blue vinyl bench seats paired with tables made of faded blue linoleum and trimmed with polished chrome sat across from a bar lined with stools. "Love Me Tender" played on the speakers. It always smelled of fresh coffee and pie and other baked goods that were proudly displayed in cases along the bar.

Jason held the door for Amanda and as he stepped inside, he took a deep breath and sighed. Coming here after work always made him relax.

It was one of his favourite places in Boston. It felt like home, cozy and warm.

"Hey, Jase," the waitress called when he appeared from behind Amanda. "Who's yer friend?"

"Oh hey, Marge. This is Amanda."

"Well, welcome to Del's. Finest pie in Boston."

Amanda smiled and inhaled deeply. "I believe that."

"You a friend of Jason?" Marge said with a grin and a wink.

Amanda smiled back, "A friend. Hopefully." Her eyes flicked briefly towards Jason as she spoke and while Jason was oblivious, Marge didn't miss the look.

"Ahhh," was all she said with a nod as she led them to Jason's regular corner booth by the big picture windows, where he could sit and watch the world outside while he ate, next to the ancient jukebox. With practised efficiency she set the faded blue linoleum table, placing paper placemats in front of them and giving each a set of cutlery. She finished off by placing a plastic covered menu before Amanda, stood up, smoothed her apron and said, "What can I get you folks?"

Amanda looked puzzled. "Doesn't Jason get a menu?"

Marge laughed, "Oh honey, he knows our menu better than I do." She turned to Jason and continued, "Your usual?"

"Sure thing," Jason smiled and looked at Marge.

"What's his usual?"

"That would be the house special. It's a classic bacon cheeseburger platter, a cola and a piece of cherry pie."

"That sounds great. I'll have one, too."

"Gotta warn yah, it's got chipotle mayo that the cook makes here. It's got some kick."

"I'm okay with kick."

"What do you want to drink?"

"Root beer, please."

"Perfect." Marge turned away and called out "Del? Burn two for the special and a couple of frog sticks."

Amanda gave Marge a concerned look as the waitress walked to the soda fountain and poured their drinks. "That isn't what we ordered."

Jason laughed. "It's diner lingo. It means burger and fries."

"Diner lingo?"

"Yeah. Diners have their own lingo. You've had to have heard it before."

Amanda looked at him blankly and shook her head.

"How haven't you heard of it?" Jason laughed. "It's like verbal shorthand. So, if someone orders two poached eggs on toast, you'd hear the cook call it Adam and Eve on a raft."

"Strange. Why do they do that?"

"Dunno. Seems like it's always been that way."

Amanda looked at Del's burly figure as he bustled about the kitchen, putting everything together. "So, making up names for things with names already is a diner thing?"

"I think it's just a thing people do." Jason chuckled, "Where are you from that you've never heard it?"

"Ahhh. I'm…" she hesitated. "I'm from Canada."

"They have diners in Canada. I've been to Halifax, Toronto, and a few other places. They all had diners."

"I'm sure not all towns have diners." Amanda fidgeted. "I'm from a very small town. Not many places to eat out."

"That's too bad. I mean about the not eating out much, not the living in Canada." Jason laughed awkwardly. "Diners have some of the best food."

"Why thank you, darlin'," Marge interrupted as she placed their drinks before them, two iced tumblers covered in condensation.

Jason took a sip and shivered from the chill.

"Thanks, Marge."

"You're welcome. Food will be up soon." She turned and headed back behind the counter.

"Well, I guess I'll find out soon just how good your diner food is." Amanda inhaled deeply. "I don't usually eat meat but that smells really good."

"No meat? If you'd said, they could have gotten you a veggie burger. They have them."

"No. It's okay. I used to be a vegan, but some things in my life changed."

"Nothing bad I hope?" Jason looked concerned.

"No. Just some changes that caused me to re-evaluate my nutrition." Amanda shrugged.

"Cool. As long as you're happy."

She nodded and they lapsed into first date awkward silence. Jason stared out the window, watching the occasional car go by while Amanda swirled the straw around in her drink. After a few minutes of staring at the paper placemats in front of them, Jason broke the silence. "Soooo…" Jason began, "you're Canadian?"

Amanda was startled. She'd been lost in her own thoughts. "No. I'm American."

"You said you were from Canada." Jason looked confused.

"What?" Amanda looked perplexed before responding, "Oh, right. Yes, I'm sorry. I was born in Canada, but my family moved here when I was a teen. I'm an American citizen."

"Okay. Gotcha. Canada's cool. Like I said, I've been there a few times. You said you were from up north. Where up north?"

"You'll not have heard the name. We don't even have a dot on Google maps."

"Damn, that is remote. What had you guys living in such an isolated area?"

"My Dad's a researcher." Amanda didn't look at Jason as

she spoke. She stared at the paper placement and spun her fork in circles.

"Your Mom?"

"She's an artist. She loved working with the local Indigenous artists."

"What did you do?" The conversation was interrupted when Marge showed up and placed the food in front of them. Amanda took this chance to change the topic.

"Thank you." She looked up at Marge and smiled, "This smell so good."

"You're welcome, sweetie."

"Thanks Marge. Thank Del for us, too."

"Will do," she said as she walked away.

Amanda took a bite of the burger and grinned, "So gwood."

Jason nodded and smiled back.

For a while they didn't talk much, just focused on their food. Jason was starved from working all night and wolfed his burger down.

Amanda matched him bite for bite.

"So, I've told you a little about me. Your turn."

"Not much to tell really. I'm from Boston. My folks live just outside of town. I live nearby in a crappy little apartment in Mission Hill. I go to MIT and I work where you met me."

"MIT huh?"

"Yeah."

"What are you studying?"

"I'm doing a computers program. You?"

"Biology. Genetics. I'm working on my masters."

"Wow. You've got your BSc already. That's impressive." Jason laughed self-deprecatingly. "I feel like a slacker."

Amanda smiled at him, her eyes sparkled, and Jason's heart skipped a beat. "Don't. I was lucky."

"More smarts than luck."

"That is luck. I did nothing exceptional to deserve intelligence. I was born like it; to me, that's luck."

"Okay, that's fair. You won the genetic lottery. But you made the most of it. Not everyone does that."

Amanda just shrugged.

"Anyway, I think it's impressive."

"Thanks."

At that moment, like magic, Marge rematerialized beside them holding a tray that bore coffee and pie. She removed their now empty plates and replaced them with dessert, then disappeared again.

"She's good," *Amanda said.*

"Yep. Love this place."

They chatted as they ate, discussing nothing of importance: funny cat videos, the weird weather and so on. When they'd finished eating Jason walked Amanda home. It was dawn by the time they got there.

"I had fun," *Jason said. He was feeling awkward again.*

"I did too," *Amanda replied.* "Give me your cell."

Jason handed it over. "What are you doing?"

Amanda handed it back to him, screen up. It was open on the contacts app and it read: "Amanda B. 617-555-4319."

"Thanks." *Jason was grinning again.*

"Can I have yours?" *Amanda returned the smile.*

"Sure." *He took her phone and put his info in.*

After a moment of awkward silence Amanda took a step up on the stairs leading to the brownstone where she lived. "Good night."

"*Good morning, you mean.*" *Jason stifled a yawn.*

Amanda laughed; it echoed around the empty street. "Text me?"

"*For sure.*"

With that she disappeared behind the heavy wooden door and Jason headed home.

It was full daylight by the time he got home and crawled into bed, but he could not sleep. Jason lay there tossing and turning for hours. Whenever he closed his eyes, he saw her face, those eyes a shade of blue like a tropical ocean.

He replayed the whole evening over and over. Criticized every stupid thing he'd said or done. He rewrote it with a much more suave version of himself, then he'd snort at his own ridiculousness and roll over only to play the scenario out a different way. He kept this up for hours until he finally dozed off, having convinced himself she'd given him a dummy number.

He awoke a few hours later to his phone buzzing. A low sun cast his room into a rainbow of reds, oranges, and purples. He'd slept the day away. Clumsily he scrabbled for his phone and flicked the screen as he rubbed the sleep from his eyes. He had three unread messages, all from Amanda B. He smiled sleepily. Maybe he would see her again.

CHAPTER THREE

"Heya, darlins," Marge drawled as Jason and Amanda stepped inside the warmth of Del's.

"Your usual table?"

"Yes please," Jason responded.

He and Amanda kicked the snow from their boots and followed Marge to their corner table by the windows as they pulled off their heavy winter jackets.

"The usual?" Marge asked.

"Ye–" Jason began.

"Actually Marge, can we see a menu please?" Amanda cut in.

Marge looked surprised but nodded and grabbed a pair from the counter. "I'll give you folks a couple of minutes to peruse and be right back." Marge headed off to tend to her other customers, leaving Jason and Amanda alone.

"Why aren't we getting the usual?"

Amanda looked at Jason and smiled, "Let's try something new."

Jason looked skeptical but picked up the menu. "How about the Double Decker?"

"Ugh, so much cheese and bacon."

"What's wrong with cheese and bacon?"

"Nothing, if you want a heart attack."

Amanda looked at Jason before she continued, "We've been saying we need to eat healthier."

"But this is Del's..."

"I know it's Del's, and they have some lovely salads on the menu."

"But–"

"At least take a look." Amanda flipped the laminated menu over and slid her finger down the list of soups and salads. "Here we go, look at this one, The Spinach Special. It has spinach, strawberries, almonds, and red onion with a raspberry vinaigrette. Or this one, The Killer Kale with fresh crisp kale, goat cheese, cherry tomatoes, mixed berries and toasted nuts with a balsamic reduction."

She looked up and Jason was making a rabbit face at her. "Seriously?"

"C'mon babe, it's Del's. Burgers and fries. Onion rings. Pie."

Amanda smiled. "Or..."

Jason looked at her skeptically.

"We have a nice healthy lunch and we can get ice cream to go for desert. We can take it for a walk through the park."

"I guess–"

"Great," Amanda chirped with a smile.

"So, you two decide yet?" Marge cut off any further debate.

"We'll have two of the Killer Kales and sparkling waters."

Marge looked from Amanda to a dejected looking Jason, who attempted a cheerful grin but instead looked a little sick, "You sure?"

Jason nodded. "Yes ma'am. We're trying to eat healthier."

"Alrighty then. It won't be long." Marge bustled away, bringing the order slip over to Del. Jason saw Del look at the *order and then over at the pair. He caught Jason's eye, raised his eyebrows and mouthed, "What the fuck?" Jason smiled sheepishly, pointed to Amanda, and shrugged. Del rolled his eyes.*

Amanda had been oblivious to the whole silent interaction. While they were waiting, she'd started flicking through the pages of a newspaper another customer had left behind.

"Did you see this?" Amanda handed the newspaper to Jason.

"What?"

"All of it."

Jason leaned over the table and looked at the headlines to see what had been so upsetting. Nothing jumped out. It was all the usual type of stuff: an article on some scammers taking advantage of the elderly, an Amber Alert for an abducted three-year-old, a convenience store shooting and so on.

"What kind of a society treats its people in such a fashion?"

Jason wasn't sure where this was going.

He hazarded a guess: "A crappy one?"

"Yes, a very crappy one." She looked both hurt and angry.

"I agree. Too many people see others as easy prey. There are sick people in this world."

"Something needs to be done about them."

"That's why we have police."

"They are inefficient at stopping crime."

"They can't stop everything before it happens. That's not realistic. They're only human. They can't see the future." Jason frowned as he looked at Amanda. This wasn't the date he'd been hoping for. "You seem pretty upset over this."

"I am. If I ever saw anything like this happen…" She trailed off and sat there, glowering at the paper as if willing a criminal to appear so she could deliver justice.

"Violence doesn't resolve anything," Jason said after a brief

pause. He wasn't sure it was the wisest thing to say but he felt he had to say something.

"Do you think any of those criminals would listen to reason?"

Jason shook his head. "No. Probably not, but vigilantes are as much a bane as boon."

Amanda shifted her eyes from the paper to Jason. "So what would you do if you saw someone being attacked?"

"Jason's a lover, not a fighter," Marge cut in as she put their drinks on the table.

Jason blushed. "I try to live by the motto 'Violence is the last refuge of the incompetent.'"

"Who said that?" Marge asked.

"It's a quote from one of my favourite authors, Isaac Asimov."

She looked at him blankly.

"He wrote the Foundation series."

Another blank look.

"How about I, Robot?"

"Is that the movie with that handsome Will Smith in it?" Marge asked while Amanda looked at him bewildered.

"Yes. Sort of. Asimov wrote the book the movie was based on."

"Hrmm, I might have to read it," Marge said.

Jason didn't have the heart to tell her the book was completely different from the movie.

"I'll loan you my copy if you want."

"Thanks. Your meals will be right up." Pen and pad in hand, Marge stepped over to the next table to take their order.

Amanda had fallen silent during Marge's discussion and when Jason turned back to her she was staring out the window, watching the people passing by.

He took a sip of his drink before he spoke.

"You okay?"

"Yes." She turned to look at him. "You didn't answer my question. What would you do?"

"Honestly, I don't know. It would probably depend on the situation."

"Scenario: You are walking home from work and you see someone trying to rob an elderly woman."

Jason thought for a minute, "First I'd call 911. Then I'd try to scare the attacker off by running towards them and yelling that I'd called the cops."

"Would that work?"

"Hopefully," Jason said with a shrug.

"If it didn't?"

"I'd put myself between the old lady and the mugger. Tell her to run. Maybe try to reason with the guy."

"You'd allow the robber to hurt you?" Amanda's brows were furrowed.

"If it meant her getting away, yeah. I'd like to think I'd do this. I hope I never have to find out."

Amanda said nothing for a while. She sat there in silence, frowning at her glass as she sipped her drink. Jason didn't interrupt her. He knew this was what she did when she was mulling over something.

"Your solution is different than what most people would do."

"Probably."

"I think I like it."

She looked up and smiled at Jason. It lit up her whole face, turning his insides to pudding. He was saved from having to come up with something else to say by Marge, who had arrived with their food.

CHAPTER FOUR

The bus jostled as it hit a pothole, snapping Jason back to the present. He looked around blearily and rubbed his hands over his eyes. They were passing the barred-up gas station, which meant they were not even halfway to work, and the bus was filling with familiar commuters. He saw the goth girl who worked at the mall on his route, the pimpled kid who worked at the fast-food place and always smelled of French fries and then he saw the creepy, grey haired, animal print wearing, cougar who hit on every person between twenty and forty. She worked at the seedy adult movie store and the bus would give a collective sigh whenever she got off. Jason looked at his watch and sighed. As he looked back up, he saw the cougar turn her head his way. He dropped his head down and closed his eyes before she had a chance to see he was awake.

A smile came over his face as he slipped back into the comforting embrace of his memories.

Jason had gotten some time off for this year's Fourth of July. They spent the evening with his parents, eating barbeque and reminiscing about Jason's childhood. They never failed to embarrass him. As a matter of fact, Jason was certain they took pleasure in doing so. Their favourite, which they told with a particular glee, was the first story they'd told Amanda. They didn't even build up to it this time. It was their opening salvo.

Jason's Mother leaned forward over her empty plate and took a sip of wine. "Every summer, we'd vacation in Nova Scotia. That's in Canada." Amanda nodded and smiled, flicking a bemused look to Jason. "Every year we'd visit the Maritime Museum. It's Jace's favourite." His Mother gave him her most proud Mom look. "This summer there was a display on the history of deep-sea diving-"

"Speaking of deep-sea diving, did you see the news from the Sea or Cortez? Something about a new species of shark..." Jason cut off his mother's story, trying to redirect it to something nice and safe and neutral, like politics or religion. He failed.

"It was quite the exhibit. Vintage diving bells, DSV's and so on. Someone-"

"An asshole." Jason grumped.

"**Someone**..." His Mother paused and shot her son a look, "...had animated an old bubble headed diving suit to activate when people walked by." Jason's mother laughed, "That person was Jason. The arms reached for him and he got such a fright that right there, in front of the tour group, he screamed and peed himself." She pulled out a photo of six-year-old Jason, wet pants and pink faced by the diver.

"Mom! Did you prep for this?" Jason said, flushing red. His Mother smiled, "Of course not dear. I always keep this picture with me."

"She does." His Father said with a grin.

"Mom..." He rubbed his hands over his burning face.

Amanda laughed and grinning at Jason before adeptly changed the conversation to his high school years.

Now his dating life, or lack thereof was up on display but at least it wasn't baby pictures.

Once the sun had set and darkness covered the city, they set off fireworks. He loved the look on Amanda's face as she watched the colourful display of willows, palms and comets as they lit up the sky. It was almost childlike in wonder. If he didn't know better, he'd have thought she had never seen fireworks before.

Afterwards, he gave her a necklace for their one-year anniversary. A coal black pendent made of meteoric iron wrapped in titanium wire and hung on a simple silver chain. He'd had it made from a small meteor he found when he was a kid. She loved it.

They returned home to their apartment and were curled up on the sofa watching Independence Day when she threw her first curveball at him.

"Babe, your Mom and I were talking today."

"Uh oh," he said, grinning.

She shot him a look, so he continued,

"About what?"

"Wanderer's."

"What about it?"

"We think you should get a different job."

Jason was surprised. He knew his Mom didn't like the place and she'd often suggested he work somewhere else. She had this irrational fear the place was going to get him killed, but he hadn't expected his Mom and girlfriend to team up on him.

"We just want what's best for you," Amanda continued.

"But I like the bar."

Amanda's nose wrinkled in distaste. "It's gross. It smells. The people are nasty and you're always getting hit on."

"Danny is only horsing around. He's not interested in me,

he's got a boyfriend," *Jason said as he put his arms around her waist, pulling her close.*

Irritated, she pushed away and moved to the other end of the sofa. *"I don't care. What about those cougars that have their eyes on you?"*

"The Tequila Sisters?" Jason chuckled at the absurdity, "Bev and Donna? Hon, they're in their seventies."

Amanda shook her head and scowled, *"No. The one who always wears the skin-tight pleather pants and leopard print blouse."*

"Dotty?"

She nodded.

"You seriously consider her a threat? She drinks like a fish, smokes two packs a day and smells like mothballs. I'd sooner sleep with Danny." Jason leaned back and looked at Amanda. "Jealousy isn't a good look."

Amanda shot him a glower that made him reconsider the wisdom of his last words.

Hastily he added, *"I know you can't seriously be jealous of women old enough to be my mother."*

With a sigh, Amanda said, *"No. I'm not jealous. I just want better for you."*

"I like the bar and some of those 'nasty people' are my friends."

"You need better friends." It was Amanda's turn to realize she'd stepped over a line. As Jason opened his mouth to respond, she cut him off, "I don't mean Duke and Bear. They're okay. I just mean friends that won't keep you away from me all night." She paused for a moment. "Or grab your ass."

Jason choked back what he'd planned on saying. Instead deciding to take a different approach, *"I make good money off the* tips."

"Only because you let the old women grope you."

"They do not grope me."

Amanda gave him a withering look.

"Okay, so not often and the ladies only get touchy if they've had too much. Even then they usually only grab my arm or touch my chest."

"Dotty. Two weeks ago."

"That was an exception. She'd forgotten she'd taken her pills before drinking. She was pretty wasted."

"Doesn't mean I have to like watching her grab at your ass."

"It's kind of flattering..." Jason began, joking, but quickly retraced those steps when he saw Amanda's expression. She could have melted steel with that look. "I mean to say, it's terribly objectifying."

Amanda huffed at his response. "You seem to enjoy it a little too much."

"I do not."

"You play up to them."

"Well, it's kind of part of my job. To make them feel... well, needed or special or wanted or something."

"It's a shitty job that expects you to allow someone to paw at you."

Jason sighed. "Amanda, I'm not going to argue this with you. I know it's a dive. It's not a high-end martini bar in the downtown area. The patrons expect a certain level of lewdness."

"Which is why you shouldn't work there. You're better than that."

"Well, if not Wanderer's, where do you recommend I get a

job to?" Jason said in exasperation.

"CloneZone."

"With you?" Jason was a little surprised.

"Why not? It's a nice, respectable office."

"It's a call centre."

"It's a printing company."

"It's a call centre," Jason repeated.

"That's only a small portion of what we do. You know that. The biggest part of the operation is the printing for our corporate clients. We do tons of instructional materials, brochures, flyers, business cards, whatever needs printing. It's so much better than that bar." She said "bar" like it was a dirty word.

It was Jason's turn to scowl. "There are good people who go to that bar."

"They are beneath you."

"Do you know that Duke is an engineer and that Butch is a minister as well as a physicist?"

"So?" Amanda stood and walked to the window, pulled back the curtain and looked out at the city skyline.

"You're judging people because of how they look, not who they are. Get to really know them, Amanda. They could surprise you."

She gave a sigh before allowing the curtain to fall back into place. "Fine" She looked over her should at Jason, her lips drawn in a tight line. Stay working there. See if I care." With that she turned on her heel and went into the bedroom, shutting the door behind her.

Jason sighed and poured himself a whiskey, thinking this was the end of the discussion. It wasn't.

The next day Amanda tried a different tactic. She spent the day sighing and when evening rolled around, she ordered in

Thai for them, cracked a bottle of wine and came out of the bedroom wearing a sexy dress she'd bought earlier that day.

"I wish we could do this every night," she said, sipping the
chardonnay.

"Mmm." Jason murmured as he rubbed her legs. They were
sitting on the sofa with the fireplace channel on the television.
Amanda was leaning back with her legs laid out across Jason,
who was slumped down with his head back and eyes closed.
He was full and just a little heady from the wine. "It would be
nice."

He felt Amanda pull her legs away and he opened his eyes
to find her staring back, pinning him in place with her look. She
leaned in and kissed him, long and passionately as she began to
unbutton his shirt. "We could make that happen." She ran her
fingers lightly over his chest and kissed his neck. He shuddered
under her touch. "Mhmmm," he replied as he pulled her against
him, and they tumbled to the floor.

Later that night they lay together on the floor, a couple of
throw pillows propped under their heads and a throw blanket
draped over them. Amanda had her head tucked into Jason's
shoulder. She could feel him breathing and hear the steady
thump of his heart against her cheek. He made her feel special
when she was with him. Safe. Happy. Something she'd never
felt before and she didn't know how to deal with these feelings.
It was the truth when Amanda had said she'd love to spend more
time with him.

"Babe? You awake?"

"Hmm?" Jason replied sleepily.

"I want this every night."

"Sounds exhausting, but I'm game to give it a try." He
smiled with his eyes closed.

He could hear the disappointment in her voice when she replied, "But we can't. You're either at work or in school. When you aren't, I am. I wish we had similar schedules."

Sighing, Jason opened his eyes and looked down at Amanda. She was on her back now, looking up at the ceiling of their little apartment. The light from the television fireplace flickered over her face and reflected off the tears in her eyes.

"Aw fuck," Jason said under his breath.

He knew he'd been played—and well. "Fine."

Amanda's eyes turned towards Jason.

"Fine?" she asked far too innocently.

"Yeah, fine. I'll apply to CloneZone tomorrow."

Amanda squealed and threw her arms around his neck, pressing herself hard against him as she kissed him.

"You won't regret this," she said as she pulled him back down, and for that night Jason had zero regrets.

Those would come later.

CHAPTER FIVE

The squealing and popping from the old bus's brakes as it stopped startled Jason from his reverie. Joe always did Jason a solid by stopping across the street from the worn-out building that held the call centre. It saved Jason's ass since the nearest official stop was nearly a quarter mile in either direction. He shivered a little as he crawled out of his seat. His clothes had begun to dry a little, but they were still damp, badly wrinkled, and there was a wet spot on the front of his pants where water had soaked in from his backpack. He looked like he'd slept in his clothes and peed himself. Sighing, he thought, "Glad I'm not trying to impress anyone."

"Have a good one," he said as he passed by Joe and his new friend Frank. He hopped off the bus and ran across the deserted rain-flooded parking lot to the main doors. Water splashed him with every step. The building had been converted from a warehouse to a large open-concept office, but no extra money was spent on restoring the exterior. The years had not been kind to the red brick, and it was dingy and crumbling. The massive glass windows had been covered over with rusty, corrugated steel,

leaving only two small filth-covered windows for natural light. Jason had always felt that the closer you came
the building, the more depressed or perhaps oppressed
you felt. It had a presence, one that weighed you down. "I
need a different job," Jason thought as he ducked under
the small overhang that sheltered the double glass doors.

He fumbled through his pockets and backpack looking for his ID badge that doubled as an electronic swipe
key. With a sinking feeling he realized that he'd forgotten
it, which meant he'd have to go through Walter, the security guard, to get in.

Jason pounded on the double glass doors, trying to
catch Walter's attention. The cranky old security guard
made a point of ignoring him, continuing to watch the
show he had on his mini TV. Walter despised tardiness
and seemed to take a perverse pleasure in delaying those
that were already running late.

"When I was your age, I got to work an hour early.
Busses didn't run then, so I had to walk ten miles each
way in all kinds of weather," Walter lectured as he slowly
picked out a temporary ID badge and keyed in Jason's
name. Jason bit down hard on his tongue; anything he'd
say would only make the old man go slower.

After what felt like an eternity, Walter finally declared
the badge was ready and held it up, wagging it slowly
back and forth. Jason grabbed the ID badge and bolted for
the card swipe which would allow him access to the centre. Jason was now beet red in the face from containing his
frustration and anger. He hoped that he might still sneak
in unnoticed. As he swiped his card the machine made a
loud buzzing noise. Startled, Jason jumped back from the

obnoxious sounding machine. "What the hell?" he said as he turned back to the smug looking old man. "Walter?"

"There is a new policy. Your manager has to sign you in. What's your manager's name again? Larry? Garry?"

"It's Tony, Walter," said a defeated Jason through clenched teeth as he returned to the security counter and hung his head.

"Tony Walter? There is no manager named Tony Walter. Are you sure you haven't been terminated for repeated tardiness?" Walter asked with a sarcastic smirk on his face.

Jason closed his eyes and took a deep breath, trying to calm himself. He said through clenched teeth, "Walter, my manager's name is Tony Smythe, or Anthony Smythe if you want."

The smirk faded to a dead glare and Jason knew he was a dead man. Walter turned back to his computer and once again using the hunt and peck method, he searched for Tony's information. "Ah, yes, here he is. A most responsible young man." As he dialed Tony's extension, he looked at Jason and said, "You could learn a lot from him." Jason nearly choked on his own tongue trying not to respond as he slumped down into a worn chair as he heard Walter say, "Tony, I got me a smart mouth out here who forgot his badge. No rush."

"No hope of sneaking in now," Jason thought glumly. He sat with his legs splayed out before him. Jason realized that even though he managed to get soaked through again while running across the parking lot, the only spot that hadn't changed was the wet spot on the front of his pants. He still looked like he'd peed himself. Dejectedly,

Jason let his head flop back to rest on the top of the chair and prayed for a quick death. He was trapped in the small lobby that reeked with the smell of the sardines that Walter loved to eat while Walter harangued his captive audience with stories of his time as a postal worker, which somehow managed to also be lectures on punctuality and reliability.

It felt like an eternity until Tony arrived to drag his sorry ass into the office. "A swift execution is better than a slow one," Jason thought as he sat up to see a very surly looking Tony standing in the open doorway.

"Come," was all that Tony said as he crooked his finger, indicating that Jason should follow him. Wearily Jason got to his feet and followed behind the scarecrow-like frame of Tony into the depths of a singularly unpleasant hell; also known as the call centre production floor.

Tony's "office" was a cubicle that was slightly bigger than the rest. The only thing different about it was a laminated sign thumbtacked to the top of the cubicle that said "FLOOR MANAGER: ANTHONY SMYTHE." Regardless of its banality, Tony felt that his office was a grey felted royal seat from which he ruled his subjects with an iron fist. A modern-day Sheriff of Nottingham for the corporate Prince John; executing their orders with glee. The employees considered it more like an evil villain's lair where he plotted ways to make their lives miserable.

Jason sat in the broken rickety chair that was permanently stuck at the lowest seat level. Tony had a bad case of Napoleon complex, which meant he had to make his staff feel smaller than he was. He did that with this broken chair that his staff had to sit in because it forced them to have to look up into Tony's bulbous pale blue eyes while

Tony looked down at them over the tops of his thick-lensed glasses.

He folded his arms across his shallow chest, crinkling his pristinely white starched dress shirt, which he kept tucked into his sharply creased khaki trousers. Every pair the man owned were just a little too short for him, exposing his white sports socks over the tops of his black loafers. To Jason, Tony always looked like the quintessential used car salesman with his dark hair slicked back, making his narrow, pinched face seem bigger than it was, and he always held an expression that seemed to look mildly disgusted at everything around him. Tony was a middle-aged sycophant; a company man all the way who cared little about his employees' welfare.

Staring into those soulless eyes, Jason decided that the best defence was a good offence, so he took a deep breath and spewed, "I'm sorry I'm late but I was here on time. I forgot my ID and Walter took forever to get a temp card for me and then I had to be signed in."

Silently, Tony reached for some paperwork and sat there in the pregnant silence, occasionally looking over the tops of his glasses at Jason and shaking his head, his thin lips drawn down in a scowl. Finally, putting the papers down and shoving them towards Jason, he said in a clipped nasally voice, "It's a pathetic man who blames others for their own transgressions. Especially when they lay the blame on a dedicated employee like Walter. You've been late three times in one month. You, sir, are now on probation. Sign this notice of probationary status."

Briefly Jason wondered how long Tony had the attendance improvement forms ready to go, just waiting for this opportunity.

Desperate, Jason tried to plead his case, "But Tony, I really was here on time."

Jason kept to himself that he believed Tony had deliberately delayed the additional thirty minutes, probably while printing and filling out the probation form.

"Don't you think it's time you started taking responsibility for your own actions? I was manager at my first job by the time I was twenty-three. With a little determination and hard work, you could someday make something of yourself."

Jason's eyes flashed with anger, which almost always meant his mouth was going to start going without any engagement of the brain. "I am responsible."

"You'd never know that from your attendance."

His sense of self-preservation was sending off klaxon alarms of warning. Jason was in a battle between his brain and tongue whether he was going to tell this weasel where to go. Jason was sure he felt blood as he bit his tongue. It was a crap job but for now it paid the bills. For the second time this day he longed for his old job as a bartender.

He died a little inside, but his brain won the battle. "Tony, I try. Honestly. It's the damned bus. This one is the earliest but it's never on time."

"That is not my problem."

"Can't you give me a later shift or something?"

"No. There are no openings."

"For fuck's sake. C'mon, man. Please. Be reasonable."

"Are you implying that I am unreasonable?" He peered at Jason over the tops of his glasses. "Have I not given you multiple opportunities? I've been most magnanimous."

"That isn't what I meant. I was just sayin' that it's hard for me to get here in time for first shift with the bus the way it is." Jason held up his hands, pleading. "Tony. Please."

"Be thankful you have a job. Others aren't so lucky." He smiled, more malicious than happy. "I'll tell you what. If you promise to show up for some training today, I'll hold off on filing the performance plan."

"What training?"

Tony waved his hand, "Oh nothing drastic. Just something that might help with your situation."

Another small piece of Jason's soul shrivelled and died, but he nodded. If he lost his job Amanda would be disappointed in him and nothing was worth that, so he choked down his anger and said, "Thank you, Tony. I appreciate the chance."

"You see, I can be magnanimous. Now you'd best get to your desk. You're already quite tardy."

As Jason grabbed his gear and headed away, his step faltered as he heard Tony mutter under his breath, "I don't know what Amanda sees in that man."

His face burning and his damp cloth sticking to his body, he headed to his desk.

"'Goddamned troll fucker" Jason whispered to himself.

"What did you say?"

Jason started and flushed bright pink, looked over his should at Tony and said "Nothing, boss. Nothing at all."

Tony gave Jason a long scrutinizing stare before waiving his hand in dismissal. Jason turned back and headed towards his desk. As he walked across the call centre floor, his wet jeans chafed his legs. His body shivered, and goose flesh rose on his arms from the building's air conditioning, which chilled him to the bone.

CHAPTER SIX

Jason's desk was at the opposite end of the floor. It wouldn't take him long to get there, the room was not large. Most of the floor space in the building was set aside for the "Printing and Distribution Centre," which was separated from the call centre by a thick protective cinder block wall. Jason's feelings flicked from anger to relief to depression as he shuffled his way towards his desk. A parade of fantasies of all the different ways that Tony could meet his demise flitted through Jason's mind: Tony's tie getting caught in the shredder; a large stack of printing paper collapsing on him and squashing Tony flat like Wile E. Coyote; Tony being run over by a forklift; Tony being covered in one of the many corrosive chemicals in the printing room and screaming, "I'm melting," as he slowly dissolved; and many more. The thoughts brought a small smile to Jason's face as he passed row after row of grey walled cubicles while automatically dodging the buckets, half-filled with rain water. There were dozens of leaks in the roof and large wet circles ringed the buckets, making the industrial carpet always smell faintly of moldy corn chips.

A familiar deep voice brought Jason back to reality. "Mijo. Where are you going?"

With a small start, Jason stopped and looked over at Marc, the only real friend he had in this place, other than Amanda. Without a word he gave a small shrug as he backtracked to his station and shoved his backpack under his desk, dropped his sodden jacket over the back of his chair and plopped down into his seat.

Marc looked at his friend with concern. "Where the hell have you been man? You're almost an hour late. Tony's gonna have your head if he catches you."

Looking at his friend, Jason said, "Too late, I've been caught, and I've already served it to him on a silver platter."

"What are you talking about?"

"Dude, I was running late. Again. I forgot my badge. Again. Walter took his sweet time to get my ID badge. Then I had to wait on His Weaseliness to log me in. In short, he knew I was late. The fucker tossed around the idea of firing me or if he should put me on probation, but instead he is sending me to some stupid training thing this afternoon."

"What the fuck did you say to him?"

"I wanted to call him a soulless pencil pusher." Jason ran his hands through his hair. "Instead I begged for my job."

"Smart choice, Mijo, you are lucky to still have a job."

"I know. It just kills me to subjugate myself to him. He's a dick."

"No argument there, but unless you won the lottery last night, you need a job."

Jason nodded as he finished logging in.

"So, in more exciting news, I'm supposed to be going out with Amanda after work. She said she 'wanted to talk.'"

"Man, that phrase is the kiss of death. It's usually said right before 'It's not you, it's me.'"

"I know. When she finds out I'm in trouble with Tony again, she's probably gonna dump me for sure."

"Why would I want to do that?" said a melodic voice from behind Jason.

Jason jumped, his eyes going wide, and shot Marc a look of sheer panic. "Manda? What are you doing here? I thought you were at that hotel setting up for the job fair," Jason said, his voice shooting at least two octaves higher than normal.

"We finished setting up the booth early and I decided to come in to get some paperwork done." She frowned at him. "I've already been talking to Tony and he told me about your meeting with him this morning."

Jason swallowed a lump as beads of sweat appeared on his brow.

Amanda only smiled. "I had told him that with the right incentive you could become a very productive member of our team. I also promised him that you would be co-operative and do *any* extra training. That's why he gave you that option instead of terminating you, which is what he wanted to do." She glanced around before touching his cheek and looked deep into his eyes. "Most importantly, I promised him you'd curb your tongue." She wagged her index finger at Jason as if he were a naughty child. "You really shouldn't goad him."

Marc choked back a laugh but Amanda heard it and shot him a glare. As she turned her gaze back to Jason she smiled again, her deep blue eyes compelling him to agree. "You will? Won't you? For me?"

"Dude, you're a smart guy. So, for once, do the smart thing," whispered Marc.

Caught by the force of Amanda's will and Marc's urging, Jason quietly whispered, "Fine. Sure."

Amanda's smile broadened. "Perfect," she said, reaching down and giving Jason a quick hug. "You won't regret it."

She turned on her heel and took off back to wherever she had materialized from.

"Man, I can't believe that. You got a last-minute reprieve from the hottest governor ever. I told you she had your back," Marc exclaimed.

"Huh?" Jason asked.

"You were whining about Amanda being pissed, but she saved your ass."

"Yeah. She did. I should have said no. I wanted to say no. I hate this shit hole and I want out. The only thing that really scares me is what her reaction to me getting canned would be."

"Not wanting to disappoint your woman isn't a bad thing, my friend. It's why I still work here."

"Your wife is pretty chill though. She'd be cool with you changing jobs."

"True 'nuff, but I'd damn well better have a job lined up to go to if I ever quit or I'm a dead man. I'm sure Amanda feels the same way." Marc said taking a whiff of his sinus medication.

"You still on that crap?"

"Better than coke." Marc said with a dramatic sniff. He grinned and then shrugged. "Doc says I'm on it until the infection clears. Stuff sucks and feels weird, but at least I can smell stuff now." Marc sniffed the air and made a disgusted face, "A fact I sometimes regret. Anyway, as I was sayin', find a new job, one you emjoy and I'm sure Amanda'll be cool with it."

"Jason shook his head. "I'm not so sure about that. I think she's a lifer for this place."

He leaned back in his chair, recalling his first days at CloneZone. The warning signs were all there.

He should have made his escape then.

CHAPTER SEVEN

The call centre occupied a run-down brick building in Boston's waterfront district. The weathered red, white, and blue sign over the door read "CloneZone: Copy & Central Printing." It was a stretch of the imagination to see it as the nice respectable office Amanda had described. It wasn't the bar, but it was definitely a dive.

Jason's new manager, Tony, gave him and the other handful of newbies the grand tour of CloneZone's call centre. It should have taken five minutes, but Tony managed to drag it out to thirty. Jason had never seen someone so enthusiastic over outdated computers and grey felted cubicles before.

"Dude, if he extols the virtues of different types of printing paper one more time, I think I'm gonna scream," whispered one of Jason's new coworkers as Tony lead them to one of the classrooms. He was like a father duck with his four charges trailing behind him. This classroom would be their office for the next couple of weeks as they were trained.

Jason stifled a laugh but nodded.

The man extended his hand, "Marc Cortez." He was shorter than Jason with short black hair, olive complexion and built like a bulldozer. Solid and stocky.

"Jason Donoghue," he said, taking the other man's hand. It was a firm, confident grip.

"What did you do to end up here?" Marc asked.

"My girlfriend works here."

"Really? What's her name?"

"You might have met her. She works in HR, recruiting, Amanda Blue."

"Pretty blonde?"

Jason nodded.

"Ah, si. Yes. She hired me." Marc gave Jason an appreciative look. "Mijo, you are a lucky man."

Jason smiled and nodded.

Marc turned serious for a minute, "Is it gonna be weird working with your girlfriend?"

"No. She works in HR doing recruitment. She isn't in the office much."

"She's lucky."

"Yeah, she attends job fairs and stuff or works from home a lot." He looked over at his new co-worker. "How'd you end up at CloneZone?"

"My wife told me I'm gonna be a Papa, so I had to get a real job."

"Congrats, man. When?"

"Thanks. Next spring. I'm still in shock I think."

"I'd say. What did you do before CloneZone?"

"Maria, that's my wife, calls it being a professional student."

"Gotcha. I know a few of those from MIT. Guys who bounce from one degree to another."

"Si. That's me. You go to MIT? Nice. That's where I did my master's in anthropology. What are you studying?"

"*Computer engineering. What were you back in school for if you had your master's? Doing your doctorate?*"

"*No. I was doing a bachelor's in history.*"

"*Why?*"

"*It was interesting.*"

"*And your wife was okay with this?*"

"*No. That's why I'm here,*" Marc laughed. "*She informed me it was time I grew up. With a kid on the way I guess she's right.*"

With that the facilitator showed up and interrupted them.

"*My name is Sue, I'm your trainer. Please introduce yourselves.*"

"*I'm Jason,*" Jason said, raising his hand.

"*Marc.*"

"*George,*" said a larger man, a smile spreading over round face. He was in his middle years, his brown hair greying at his temples.

"*Jamie,*" the woman squeaked, though you could hardly hear her. She looked around at the others nervously.

"*Thank you. We'll start with a getting to know you exercise. I want you to each put something about yourselves on this piece of paper…*"

"*This is the fifth circle of hell,*" Jason thought as he scribbled something pointless on his piece of paper before Sue collected it for redistribution.

***

"*Nice sweater,*" Amanda said, laughing.

Marc grinned. "*Maria bought if for me. And I quote: 'Honey, everyone needs a cute ugly Christmas sweater.' I didn't have a choice.*"

"*I think it's cute.*"

"I dunno," Jason mumbled around his slice of cold pizza. "I think that snowman is over compensating." He pointed to the large stuffed carrot nose that was protruding from the middle of Marc's chest.

"Haha," Marc muttered as he tried to squish the proboscis back in.

"What's wrong with its nose?" Amanda asked.

Jason looked at her. "It was a joke?"

"Yeah, chuckles was trying to intimate that I am not well endowed."

"Never said anything about you, just the snowman," Jason said, laughing.

"I don't see how that's funny?"

Marc laughed as Jason said, "It was a double entendre."

Amanda just looked at him and blinked.

"Never mind," he said.

The conversation lulled as they finished their meals.

"You guys are the only reason I'm still working here," Jason said out of the blue.

"Dude, I'm with you," Marc said as Amanda sighed heavily and rolled her eyes.

She'd heard this complaint too many times.

"You've only been here less than a year.

It's a start. Work hard and you can go places."

"Where? Where can I go?" Jason shook his head. "I want to finish my degree before I turn thirty, but you seem dead set on me staying here with you. Every time I mention working any other place, you get upset." The bar wasn't good enough, even when Marge at the diner offered him a job, it wasn't acceptable. Jason looked at Amanda; there was no way she could be jealous of Marge. "Once I graduate, I can get a job with NASA or SpaceX or something. Good hours. Good money. A better job. Anything.

As long as it's not here. I can't even get back to school with the hours at CloneZone."

"I know it's not your dream job," Amanda reached over and placed her hand on Jason's, giving it a gentle squeeze. "Babe, you just need to stay positive. Good things will happen."

"I'm trying. I just don't fit here."

"Will you try to hold out a little longer? For me? There are new positions coming up that I'm sure you'd be perfect for."

"What are they?"

"Well, I'm not supposed to say yet." Amanda looked around. There was no one nearby. "There's a couple opening up in lower management and one in IT."

"What's the one in IT?"

"You'd have to be working closely with Tony. It has to do with some project he's been working on."

"That's a downside. Do you know anything more about it?"

"No. Not yet." Amanda frowned and stood to leave. "I need to get back to work."

Marc looked over at Jason. "You certainly know how to clear a table."

"It's a gift," he said.

Jason tried to keep his promise, to remain upbeat and optimistic, but the place slowly drained the life from him.

He'd grown to hate his job, his boss, the bus shelter that smelled of pee, the bus that was never warm and always late, his co-workers, the customers, the coffee machine that only worked sometimes, and the clunky old vending machines that ate your money but never gave you your nice salty pretzels. Every day he dragged himself to this soul-sucking abyss, and every day he realized he was stepping further and further away from his goals.

The call centre was where dreams went to die.

CHAPTER EIGHT

Most days, the three friends took lunch together in the dingy cafeteria. Jason sat stirring his Styrofoam cup of noodles, while Amanda nibbled on her garden salad and Marc started to wolf down his huge foot-long meatball sub, pizza sauce and cheese dripping out the sides. Jason always wondered how a guy who ate like Marc could manage to stay in such great shape.

"Just look over there," Marc pointed across the cafeteria with his elbow. One of their co-workers was sitting at a table. He had a lunch bag opened in front of him but wasn't moving. He was staring vacantly at the wall and a string of saliva dangled from his chin. "What the fuck's up with him?"

"He looks normal to me," Amanda replied, shrugging her shoulders.

"He is most definitely not normal," Marc said around a mouthful of his sub.

"Maybe he's coming down with that flu that's hitting everyone?" Amanda suggested. "Just yesterday someone reported that Lucas was sitting on the floor crying. But he wasn't." Jason and Marc both looked at her with a con-

fused expression. "I mean crying. That is, he wasn't crying. He'd been coughing and sneezing like crazy all morning. When he went on break, he got really dizzy and just
sat on the floor with his eyes all watery."

"It's a pretty brutal cold," Jason said as he started to
wolf down his cooled pot noodles.

"Yeah. At least half the centre seems to have caught
this bug. I had it just after I started. They found me asleep
in my lunch and I ended up being off sick for almost a
week," Amanda said.

"I didn't know that," Jason said, looking at Amanda.

"It was before we met," she said dismissively. "I don't
think I've ever been so sick. I was so out of it my room-
mate had to look after me."

"Smee ris rah feehin wuggy," mumbled Marc, his
mouth stuffed with sub. Both Amanda and Jason looked
at him, raising their eyebrows in unison. Washing down
his food with a gulp of soda, Marc burped and said, "Sorry. What I said was 'He is a freakin' druggy'."

The two continued to look at him, but Amanda started
to frown.

"I mean Gary is a drug dealer who uses his own prod-
uct. Everyone knows that." Marc shuddered dramatically
and burped again. "They are always bad news. I don't
trust those types." Marc gave Gary a hard look. The guy
was an addict. Something most of his co-workers knew.
Some even got their weekend weed from him. He was a
failed chemist who'd had a good job with one of the phar-
maceutical companies, but he'd taken too much of a liking
to the narcotics he'd been developing.

Both Jason and Amanda shook their heads at Marc before Jason replied, "Well, I just know I don't want whatever bug he's got."

Amanda leaned over, touching her shoulder against his, and whispered huskily, "I'll take care of you."

Marc made gagging noises around his sub while Jason flushed.

Giggling, she sat back up. "Oh. Did you get an email from Tony?"

"Who? Me?" Jason and Marc asked in unison.

Amanda laughed. "Jason."

"Yeah, he wants me to go to the training session at three. Me, Jamie, and George. The annual meeting of the CloneZone losers club," Jason replied, sighing heavily. He realized he had been sighing an awful lot today.

"Must be," Marc said, swallowing down the last of his meal and wiping his hands on a paper napkin as Jason looked at his friend with a hurt look. He hadn't expected Marc to agree quite so readily. "I got an email, too. Tony must think you are having a negative influence on me." He smiled, taking the sting from his words.

"What?" both Amanda and Jason said in unison.

"Yeah. The email didn't say what exactly the training was, just that it's you, George, Jamie, and me at three PM, in classroom two."

Amanda sat with her brow furrowed, staring at the last piece of lettuce as she moved it slowly in circles with her fork.

"You okay?" Jason asked Amanda.

"What? Oh yeah, sorry. I was just thinking about what Marc said. It's just odd that Tony didn't notify me. I have to record what training you receive, and I thought there was only three of you scheduled for today."

"Probably just a miscommunication," Jason said. "It's probably just another stupid 'attendance is important' corporate brainwashing training. We'll be told how important we are and that being late or absent causes undue hardship to our coworkers and blah blah blah. You'd think that the world was going to end if we didn't show up."

"Yeah," Marc agreed. "I always feel like I've stepped into some sort of Orwellian indoctrination nightmare when I sit through those. Maybe that is what they're really doing to us. There are some sort of sci-fi subliminal messages embedded into the PowerPoint presentation repeating 'Obey your masters' over and over."

Jason chimed in, "We're really human versions of Pavlov's dogs. Someone rings a bell and we all answer, 'Hello, how can I assist you today?'" Both men laughed. They never noticed that Amanda's face had gone a sallow green colour or when she finally slipped away.

When they finally stopped laughing at their own joke, Marc said, "Where'd Amanda go?"

Jason looked around and shrugged as he tossed his empty noodle container into the trash and the two men headed back to their desks. "Probably to find out why she was left out of the loop about that training."

"Probably."

The two men returned to their desks and returned to work. It was busy so the hours flew by and before they knew it, it was almost three PM.

Marc stood and stretched before heading off to the training session. He passed Amanda as she headed towards where they sat. "Don't worry. He's coming. He's just stuck on a call, Amanda. It shouldn't be long."

Amanda didn't even acknowledge Marc as she brushed past him.

"Thanks for the heads-up, Marc," he said in a falsetto. "You are most welcome, Amanda," he said with a shrug as he headed off to class.

Amanda heard none of it. She arrived at Jason's desk, glad to see him still sitting there. After hesitating only slightly, she sat down in Marc's vacated chair, scooted over to sit closer to Jason, and waited impatiently for the call to end. She could see he was reviewing the finalized order and wasn't really paying attention to her.

"Jason, I need to talk to you," Amanda whispered, tugging at his sleeve.

"Okay. Almost done," he mouthed back and held up his finger indicating "one minute." Jason continued to finalize a priority order for 20,000 high gloss flyers to be printed depicting a chartreuse and lavender chicken, with country western fonts; once printed they were to be shipped via courier to Pretty Chickie's Country Emporium in Bird City, Kansas. Jason was struggling to keep a straight face during the call.

"Okay then. That wasn't weird at all," Jason said, laying down his headset.

"Sup?"

Amanda turned to face Jason and took his hands in hers, looking up into his eyes. She loved they way they sparkled with intelligence and gentleness. They made her heart skip a beat every time. She knew she should not feel this way, but she could not help herself. The emotions she felt were too strong to deny.

Shaking her head, she steeled herself and shut herself to the pain that surged in her heart and said urgently, "This wasn't how it was supposed to happen. I'm sorry, Jason. I'm so sorry. Marc is gone and you need to get out of here." She paused. "Right now. You can't delay."

"Go? Where? Training? I'm going no–"

Amanda cut him off harshly. "No. Away from here. Get as far as you can from CloneZone, from Boston."

Jason looked hurt and confused. "Why? Gone? What do you mean that Marc is gone? Are you dumping me?"

"No. Yes. Just GO. Please." Amanda was near tears.

"I'm not going anywhere without an explanation."

"Of course you aren't. You are truly a stubborn asshole, Jason Donoghue." Her switch to anger was like a slap in the face to Jason and he reeled back from her a little.

"Wow."

"You are. I'm trying to sav–" Amanda cut herself off before continuing, "I'm trying to help you and you simply will not listen. Just fucking GO already!" she screeched at him as she jumped to her feet and ran out of the building.

CHAPTER NINE

Marc really did love these training sessions. A couple of hours away from the phones and the pedantic clients was a gift from above. Two sheets missing out of 300,000 printed and their world comes to a screeching halt. "Who counts those things?" he thought as he walked into the tiny classroom with its dull beige walls and row after row of tables, each holding five semi-functional computers. There was no personal space here if the class was full. Just you and twenty-nine of your new best friends. Marc was glad there were only four of them today. These rooms were always close and stuffy. It was a crap shoot if the AC was going to work.

The trainer hadn't shown yet, so Marc flopped down into one of the chairs as far back in the classroom as he could go, shifted his sinus meds as the bottle dug into his hip and then leaned back as far as the chair would go. Meanwhile his two companions were chatting quietly. Marc had mastered the call centre survival skill of napping with your eyes open and took full advantage of it in the classroom. It would be a little harder today, with so few in the class, but he was willing to give it a shot. Until he had to feign alertness, he leaned back in the rickety chair and closed his eyes.

"Jesus," Marc thought. "Jason's going to miss another class." He was just wondering if he should start a pool on who's most likely to kill Jason: Amanda or Tony. The classroom door shut with a loud bang. "Ah, there he is," Marc mumbled under his breath, opening his eyes, expecting to see Jason. There was no one there. The three of them were still the only ones in the room. "Must have been the wind," Marc muttered as he closed his eyes once again.

George got up to open the door, but the handle wouldn't turn. He jiggled it up and down then leaned hard against the door. "It won't open," he said with finality.

"Wadda yah mean it won't open?" Marc grumbled.

The racket George was making was ruining his nap. He opened one eye a crack to see George violently yanking and shaking the door while trying futilely to twist the handle. With a resigned sigh, Marc got up to help. This training course wasn't working out like he'd planned. After a few attempts of his own, he realized the door was well and truly stuck. He could see people in the distance, so he pounded on the door and the glass, but no one came; they didn't even look.

"We're trapped," Jamie squealed, her hands raising to her throat.

"We're just gonna have to wait until the trainer shows up," Marc said, but continued quickly when Jamie gave him such a look of terror. "It shouldn't be long." He glanced at his watch. "They are already fifteen minutes late."

He looked at Jamie, who was pale and sweating. She kept making small squeaking noises and looking around frantically. She reminded him of a mouse stuck in one of those little mazes that he'd seen on science programs in school. The little white critters were trapped in narrow corridors and they weren't allowed freedom until they'd solved the maze or done their master's bidding. When they did well, the reward was a scrap of cheese and a bigger cage.

Marc shook his head. His thoughts were making him feel claustrophobic. As much to himself as to the others he said, "Chill. The door's just jammed. It's happened before. Let's see if we can get someone on the office chat to come and open the door from the outside." Marc turned to the classroom's computers and sat down at the computer next to Jamie and patted her shoulder.

"It'll be okay. Won't take long for someone to come." She looked at him gratefully and tried a smile. Marc thought it just made her look sick, but he smiled back in what he hoped was an encouraging way as he turned back to the computer and wiggled the mouse. Nothing happened. He hit the power button on the computer, but still nothing happened. He tried the next three computers in a row and none of them would start.

"They're all broken?" he said, looking over at George, who'd continued to pound at the door.

"I'll check this side," George said. After four separate attempts he looked over at Marc. "These won't start either."

"What the fuck?" Marc muttered under his breath. He took out his cell phone to call someone. "Of course. No fucking reception," he said, looking at the four empty little bars. "Goddamned concrete."

He looked at Jamie, who was pale and sweating. She was curled up tight but was making furtive little movements with her hands and feet, while her wide eyes flicked from Marc to George to the door. It was if she wanted to run but didn't know which way was safe.

"I guess that's it. Nothing else we can do. We might as well make the best of it." Marc said, resigned and opened his phone, "Either of you got the app for Cake Layers game? We can do a team round."

Marc heard a mouse being dropped back onto the desk and George's sigh. "Guess not." He muttered just as George said, "I don't get this. None of the computers will turn on." He'd moved on from trying to find one that worked to trying to find out why they wouldn't.

"Marc?" George said. Marc turned around to look at George, who was pulling on a computer in the last row, but the machine wasn't moving. "They're bolted to the fucking desk."

As he spoke the computer tore away from the desk with a loud crack, sending George tumbling. The computer flew from his hands, landed across the room, bounced off the back wall and smashed open on the floor. Jamie screamed at the sound of metal meeting concrete.

"Dude, you okay? " Marc said as he helped George up off the floor.

"Yeah. I think so," he said, rubbing his backside.

"That thing is obliterated," Marc said. "You know, they'll probably take the cost of it out of your pay."

"Of that I have no doubt. Won't matter why it happened."

"Nope and they'll probably charge you double what

the piece of shit is worth too."

The two men stopped, looking down at a hollow box. There were no motherboard, hard drive, or memory cards in sight. Just the twisted metal frame of an empty box with a few colourful wires and empty tubing. George and Marc looked at each other.

Frowning, Marc whispered to George, "What the fuck is going on here?"

The room's lights flickered and dimmed. Jamie yelped and curled into a ball. Marc thought he heard a low hissing noise. It seemed to emanate from everywhere.

"You guys hear that?" Marc said to the others as he turned in a slow circle.

"Marc, some of the computers have lights on now," George said as he dropped into a chair in front of the nearest one and tried to get it to work. Marc looked down at the completely empty case and back at his companions.

He scrunched his nose. "Do you guys smell something? It's like lemon house cleaner or something?" He paused again, sniffed, and sneezed violently. Whatever it was it burned when he breathed. "It's like Mr. Clean but way stronger?" Marc's Spider-Sense was tingling like crazy.

Jamie gave the air a little sniff.

"Yeah," she said in a high voice. She hadn't moved from where she huddled in a chair by the door.

"Frig, my throat and eyes are burning," George said, rubbing them.

"Mine too," Jamie squeaked.

"It's giving me a headache," Marc added, rubbing his temples.

George was holding tight to the edge of the desk.

"Guys, I'm not feelin' so good. Anyone else feeling dizzy?"

Both Marc and Jamie nodded.

"Carbon monoxide?" Marc suggested. The building was heated by a furnace, but it hadn't been on in weeks due to the heat. It was getting harder and harder to think.

"Guys, look at this." George's speech slurred as he lifted the end of a piece of flexible metal conduit piping that had been attached to the dummy computer. He was still rubbing his eyes with his free hand and coughed. What looked like a faint wisp of smoke wafted lazily from the open end and drifted towards the tile ceiling.

"It's empty..." was all he managed. George gagged and fumbled at the desk's edge as he started to slide from the seat. He stood and took a step, but his legs collapsed beneath him and he dropped to his knees. He looked plaintively at Marc and Jamie while his mouth moved but no words came out. His eyes rolled up into his head and he flopped the last few feet to lie on the floor, hitting his head on the desk's edge on the way down.

"What's wrong with him?" Jamie gasped. She was finding it hard to breathe.

The room was starting to spin. Marc's stomach rolled, and he fought the urge to throw up.

"Gas..." Marc said in a slurred voice as he looked at the humming computers. His vision dimmed as he dropped to his knees. Jamie never heard his answer. Never once moving from her chair, she now slid to the floor. Her head hit the carpet-covered concrete floor with a thunk.

Fighting against the gas, Marc tried to make it to the door. As his fingers brushed the handle his unconscious form fell, pinning Jamie beneath him.

CHAPTER TEN

Jason bolted after Amanda, brushing past a startled Walter who glowered at Jason's back as he disappeared through the doors. The old curmudgeon didn't hesitate to head to his computer to report what he'd seen to his favourite manager.

The rain was still coming down as Jason ran across the parking lot, scanning the horizon for Amanda. "Where could she have gone?" he thought. He stood in the middle of the parking lot looking as far up the street as he could, across the series of linked parking lots and along the waterfront's edge. Which route had she chosen? He was frozen with indecision while hundreds of scenarios tumbled through his mind. He looked at the water lapping against the piers. They often walked along those piers during lunch. She said she found the water soothing. He took a chance that was where she'd go, so he headed across the lot and began jogging along the water's edge.

As he jogged, the rain stopped, leaving a stifling humidity that gave a potency to the cornucopia of fragrances that proximity to the waterfront provided. The air smelled of damp, mixed with tang of salt from the ocean, the bitterness of diesel, the stink of rotting fish with just a touch of hops from a brewery up the road. The fetid air made it difficult to breathe and his chest was beginning to hurt from his exertion.

He was relieved to see Amanda standing on one of the small piers that jutted out into the water. She was standing on the wooden beams that edged the concrete wharf, with her back to him. She was staring down into the water's murky depths. Her shoulders were slumped, and he could just see her quivering as she choked back sobs.

"Manda?" he said quietly.

As he spoke Amanda made a small yelp of surprise and spun towards Jason. As she turned, the water-soaked wood beneath Amanda's feet betrayed her and she slipped backwards, her arms windmilling in a vain attempt to regain balance. It was not enough. Looking at Jason, eyes wide with fear, she let out a silent scream and fell backwards into the sea.

Time seemed to slow as Jason watched her fall. He dove for her, tried to grab her outstretched hand, but the distance was too great. Amanda slipped away from him. He heard the splash as she hit the water ten feet below the pier's edge. A new fear gripped Jason, freezing him where he stood.

He couldn't swim.

The impact drove what little breath Amanda had from her lungs, stunning her. Warm water enveloped her as she sank, wrapping her in a peace that drew her in, comforting her. She could see a watery sun above as it tried to break through the clouds. Bits of flotsam passed overhead, breaking the fractal beams that penetrated the water. Her lungs burned. They cried for air but found only the briny water that had filled them.

"This is for the best," she thought as she closed her eyes and succumbed to the sea. This was a far better fate than being forced to choose between her two worlds.

Then Jason was there, wrapping his arms around her as he held her tight and fought to drag them both to the surface.

"I'm gonna die," he thought, "but at least I tried."

Rough waves hit Amanda's face as they broke the surface. Air tried to force its way into her water-filled lungs. She choked and coughed hard.

"No," she tried to scream at Jason, but it came out as a garbled moan as gouts of sea water poured from her tortured lungs. She fought weakly against his grip, but he held tight and frantically pulled her to the wharf's edge. Jason grabbed hold of one of the barnacle-encrusted pilings, holding tight while the sharp shells made tiny painful cuts on his palm.

She fought vainly to pry his arm from around her waist, kicking against his legs. "Stop," he cried, choking as a wave washed over his head. "You'll kill us both." She looked over her shoulder. He was terrified as he struggled to get them out of the water. He was exhausted and struggled to hold onto the slimy beams as the strong current pulled at them. His hand slid along the wood, the barnacles cutting his hands. Each wave threatened to tear them away and pull them under. Reluctantly she stopped her struggles and took hold of the pier while treading water.

"Let me go," Amanda finally managed. Her voice was a raspy croak. "Save yourself."

"No," was all he said. Frantically he searched for a way to get them out of the water. Wood and concrete surrounded them. He finally spotted a ladder on the pier opposite them.

"There's our way out," he said. "You need to help me get us there. I can't do it alone."

Amanda only nodded.

Jason pushed away from their precarious perch. The pier was forty feet away, but it might as well have been miles. Jason looked like a drowning moose; arms and legs flailing, gulping in the filthy harbour water, making him choke and gag. Amanda used what little strength she had left to assist. Together they fought against the waves and a current that tried to pull them out to sea. Jason was surprised when he felt his hand touch the rusty metal.

He swung Amanda around in front of him, helping her get a grip on the ladder's rungs. He watched as she climbed out ahead of him, collapsing facedown on the ground when she reached the top. Moments later Jason fell alongside of her, collapsing in exhaustion.

After they'd cleared themselves of all the sea water in their lungs they lay together on the wharf; Jason's arm was draped lifelessly across Amanda's shoulders. How long they lay there, Amanda didn't know. His arm was warm against her and she could feel his breathing returning to normal. She didn't want to move. She knew once the contact was broken, reality would return, time would start moving forward again, and she'd have to face him.

Suddenly Jason sat up, pulling his arm away. The separation was jarring. Amanda lay there, keeping her eyes closed.

"Manda?" he said quietly. "I know you're awake." He reached out and touched her shoulder. Amanda pulled away roughly and stood, walking a few steps away before stopping.

"Amanda," he said more insistently.

"Please. No."

Jason stood and walked around her, and she turned with him, keeping her back to him until she was facing the sea. The wind had picked up a little and waves crashed against the pier. It made her shiver. She was soaked and the wind was chilling her, but that didn't matter.

"Amanda, you have to talk to me," Jason pleaded.

"Why can't you just trust me? You need to leave. Go as far as you can as fast as you can."

Jason paused as he looked at her. She looked resigned or defeated; he wasn't sure anymore.

"Are you trying to dump me?"

"No," she said, shaking her head.

Her wet hair whipped her face, stinging.

"Yes. Oh, please Jason, just go."

"You want me to drop everything and leave. No, explanation, no reason." Jason paused. "That's crazy."

"You have no idea."

"I would, if you'd talk to me."

She said nothing, just stood there staring at a flock of gulls that bobbed up and down on the waves. She thought them fortunate. Free.

"Amanda?"

She shivered and took a deep breath, held it, and with a slight sigh let it out all in one breath.

"You'll never believe me."

"Let me be the judge of what I will and will not believe. I can be pretty open minded. 'There are more things in heaven and earth, Horatio, than are dreamt of in your philosophy.'"

"Hamlet?" Amanda said, looking up to the horizon. "I didn't know you knew Shakespeare."

"There are a lot of things you don't know. Now, give me a chance," said Jason.

"I can't."

"If you want me to leave, you have to trust me enough to tell me the truth."

CHAPTER ELEVEN

Marc's eyes fluttered as he fought his way back to consciousness. His head throbbed horribly, and his mouth felt like something large and fuzzy had died there about a week ago. With a groan he tried to sit up but brought up solid against the restraints that held him to the bed. "What the fuck?" he muttered as he tugged against the heavy bindings. There were three heavy leather straps: one across his lower legs, another across his hips, with the last across his chest. He felt sick to his stomach and tried to look around, but he could see almost nothing.

He fought back panic. Where was he?

What was happening? Why was he naked? Thoughts of all those stupid conspiracy theory and alien abduction shows he'd watched flitted through his befuddled brain. They were right? Had he been probed? He ran his thumb over his hand. "Nope, no implants," he thought. None that he could feel anyway. The strap across his chest was a little loose, so with effort he was able to wriggle his elbows under his body and prop himself up a little, giving him a little bit better view of where he was. His initial relief at the dim lighting was washed away in a need to see his surroundings. "The fuckers have taken out my contacts," he growled under his breath, squinting myopically as he peered into the shadows.

He could just make out two forms, one to his right and one to his left, both lying on tables of their own. Marc glared up at the few dim pot lights around the ceiling as if he could make them brighter. They cast a ghostly light down on the prone figures. The Force was not with him and the lights didn't get any brighter.

Marc squinted into the darkness on his right. He was pretty sure it was George; his unclothed rotund form lay unmoving on what looked like a hospital gurney. Leather restraints lay alongside George's immobile form and his arms hung limply over the sides. Marc thought he saw what looked like trickles of dark brown dried blood that had run from George's eyes and ears, forming a small pool just beneath his jaw.

"Fuck," Marc whispered. He lay back, closing his eyes against the horror. What the hell had happened? Where were they? He tried to sit, but heavy straps lay across his chest, hips and legs. Thinking hurt, his brain felt like it was on fire.

If that were George on his right, Marc was sure it would be Jamie lying cold and lifeless to his left. He didn't want to see her like that.

The silence was broken by a soft whimper from his left. His heart sped up and he slowly turned his head to look. "Jamie?" he said in as loud a whisper as he dared. He couldn't see much, but a pale halo of light from one of the pot lights right above her lit her face just enough that he could see her profile. She looked terrified. Her eyes were open but locked unblinking on an invisible spot on the ceiling above her. Unlike George, she was still retrained, and her hands were clenched tightly into fists and her whole body seemed to be quivering slightly. She looked like she was fighting an invisible battle; every now and then she'd let out another whimper. Marc didn't know if it was pain, fear, or both.

"Jamie," he said louder. Her only response was a whimper.

"Damn it. Fucking damn it," he yelled and started to fight violently against his bonds. Waves of dizziness and nausea swept over him. "Jesus help me," he prayed. He felt like he was trapped in a bizarre urban legend come to life. As his vision began to dim, he wondered that if he woke again would he wake up in a bathtub full of ice, his kidney gone, and a cell phone taped to his hand. That was his final thought as the darkness claimed him once more.

CHAPTER TWELVE

Amanda sighed as she fought back tears. She'd spent the last two years hiding in plain sight. She'd been trained in subterfuge, and now Jason wanted her to just tell everything. He had no idea what he was asking.

She turned and looked Jason in the eye. "I was going to tell you this tonight, but I guess it'll have to be now." She paused. "I love you."

"You what?" Jason asked, completely dumbfounded at this complete turnaround.

"I love you. I need you to know that before I say anything else."

"I love you too, Amanda," Jason said, smiling as he stepped forward to hug her, but she recoiled, just stopping herself from falling into the water once again. Jason stopped cold, his arms still held out before him.

"Okay," he said, lowering his arms. He sounded so hurt Amanda's heart nearly broke, but she steeled herself. She had to be strong.

"I love you, but you need to go. You need to go because I love you."

"That is about as ass-backwards a statement as I've

ever heard." Frustration was seeping into his voice now. He sounded angry and Amanda was glad to hear it.

Anger she could deal with.

"Listen to me, it's a crazy story and I don't have an ounce of proof. If you want to know the truth, I'll tell you. Once I do, do you promise to go?"

"I'll make no promise until I know why."

Amanda turned from him again.

"That will have to do, I suppose." She took one final deep breath, held it and let it out all at once, steeling herself for what she was about to say.

"I know you were doing some astronomy in school."

"Yeah…"

"Well," Amanda paused and stared at the water glistening on the ground. Tiny prisms refracting in what little light there was. "You aren't going to believe it."

"Try me."

"I don't know how to start. It's incredulous to even me."

"Just say it."

Amanda turned and looked at him over her shoulder. "How many species do you think are on Earth?"

"I dunno, lots. Maybe millions?"

"Around 8.7 million."

"That's specific."

"It is. Species of all types from bacteria that can live by volcanoes to complex creatures like homo sapiens."

"Okay." Jason nodded but looked more confused than ever. "Where is she going with this?" he thought.

"With all that diversity, do you think humans are the only sentient species?"

"Of course not," Jason answered immediately. "We have dolphins and whales as well as other primates."

Amanda hesitated before continuing, "What about single-celled species?"

"No. "

"Are you certain?"

"I'm into computers not microbes, but no, there is nothing I know of on Earth that has any real intelligence."

"What about the ones they found from Mars?"

"They were fossils in rocks. I don't know anything else about them."

"So, you believe that there could be life elsewhere?"

"Of course. So many solar systems with so many planets. It's narcissistic of us to assume to be the only intelligent life in the universe. Why?"

Amanda continued, ignoring his question. "How much do you know about the Perseids meteor shower?"

"Random."

"How much do you know?"

"I know some. It happens in August. The meteors come from the asteroid belt for the most part."

"Okay. What if I told you that of all the thousands of meteors that shower Earth during the meteor shower not all of the meteors came from the asteroid?"

"I'd call bullshit and ask how you knew."

"Let's say I heard it somewhere."

"Then I'd ask when you started getting secrets from NASA."

"This isn't from NASA."

"SETI then, or do I want to know from where?"

"Probably not, but you asked. Do you remember back

in 1993 NASA found fossilized bacteria from Mars in a meteor here on Earth?" Amanda shivered as a low ground fog crept its way forward like a predator stalking its prey. Its tendrils wrapped around them, shrouding them, giving them a sense of isolation. "How many of those meteors actually make it through the atmosphere and deposit debris or hit the Earth? And of those, how many are seen by people?

"Most likely hundreds, if not thousands, but I doubt many are seen by people. Ones like that big one that hit Russia a few years ago are rare. There's a reason meteor hunters have day jobs."

"So, do you think that it is plausible of the thousands of meteors hitting the Earth each year, some could hold life?"

"Like, alien life?"

"More or less."

"Statistically it's not likely."

"Why?"

"NASA tracks anything that doesn't come from our solar system, so they'd know if something like that came through, let alone had an impact course with Earth."

"NASA isn't infallible. They don't even have a full catalogue of all near-Earth asteroids, let alone small rocks." Amanda paused, wrapping her arms around herself, and shivered. "So, I ask again, is it possible?"

Jason stopped to think. He thought about all the things he'd read over the years. The writings of Sagan, Einstein, and Hawking. The universe was impossibly expansive. Sagan once said, "The universe is a pretty big place. If it's just us, it seems like an awful waste of space."

"Yeah, it is. Really anything is possible, but most things aren't plausible or even probable. If I apply Occam's Razor…"

"Occam's Razor?"

"You've had to have heard of it."

Amanda gave him a look of consternation.

"Occam's Razor states that the simplest explanation is usually the truth."

"Usually. Not always."

Jason nodded his acquiescence. "Fair enough. Continue please."

"The fact is some meteorites do contain active life. Most burn up in the atmosphere. No one ever knows. Others don't survive this planet."

"I'm still calling bullshit, but I do concede that Earth is a toxic place. Our nice corrosive atmosphere and water. It protects us quite well."

"Yes, it does." Amanda smiled weakly. "However, it's not perfect. A microscopic creature called a tardigrade can live quite well in multiple hostile environments right here on Earth. So why not other microbes?"

"You're saying some survive?"

"Yes. In 2008 a handful survived. They crashed into the Atlantic Ocean just off the coast of North Carolina."

"Right." Jason dragged the word out, so it sounded more like "Riiiggghhhttttt."

"It's true. No one saw its spectacular fiery entry before it impacted the Atlantic Ocean, spraying water and steam a hundred feet in the air. It broke apart as its superheated exterior hit the cooler water, dumping its contents into the sea."

"How do you know all this?" Jason asked hesitantly. She hadn't answered this question yet and he had a feeling he didn't want to hear it.

Amanda continued, once again acting as if she'd not heard him. "This little meteor didn't come from Earth's nearby asteroid. Its journey was much longer. It came from the solar system called 70 Virginis."

"Okay, I'll play along. How frigging long did it take the space rock to get here?"

"If it had flown by itself? Billions of years. Six hundred and ten, to be exact."

Jason gave her an incredulous look.

"Fuck."

"Yes. Very much fuck. Some species are far more patient than others."

"How frigging far away is the Virgin system?"

"It's 70 Virginis, and it's around seventy-eight light-years from Earth."

"So, you are saying that bacteria survived for that long?"

"This species did. That little rock held an occupying force."

"A what? How?" Jason was skeptical.

"Thousands of the rocks were sent out from the Virginis system. The rocks didn't have propulsion systems as such. They were shot from a space station that orbited Acantha. Each given a destination planet that was thought to hold life. They could use outgassing for small manoeuvres. Newtonian physics was their best bet."

Jason nodded, getting caught up in the story. "An object in motion remains in motion unless acted upon by an outside force."

"Exactly. Like the gravity of a solar system. It slowed the rock, and the small gas jets allowed its occupants to align its trajectory with Earth."

"I'd love to study this rock." Jason was sure Amanda was having a go at him. No way was this true, and, if it were, there was no way for her to know.

Now that she'd started talking, she couldn't seem to stop. "It was a crap shoot that they would make it to a viable planet. Most probably never did."

Jason stood looking at Amanda's back, the fog twisting and rolling between them. She was shrouded in a cloak of mist; pale, with wisps of her drying fair hair fluttering in the wind, she looked like a wraith. The fog held her every word, letting it linger. Jason shuddered.

She took a breath before continuing. "Acanthans are similar to Earth's amoeba but their unique cellular structure allowed them to hibernate in the frigid temperatures of space, it protected against the hellish heat of re-entry and then the highly corrosive salt water. Remember tardigrades?" She gave him another deadpan stare.

"Alright. I get it. Who named them?"

"They named themselves."

"Amanda, I know I've said this before, so at the risk of sounding repetitive, I have to say again, bullshit."

"No bullshit, Jason. I promise."

"I asked for the truth and you give me some sci-fi bullshit answer. If you wanted to break up, you should have just said so." He was angry. "You didn't have to go to these lengths."

"I didn't want to break up with you."

"Didn't?" Jason looked angry and hurt.

"I don't."

"That's not how it looks to me."

"I promise. You wanted the truth. I'm telling you the truth," Amanda snapped, her own anger coming to the surface. "You promised me you'd keep an open mind."

Jason gave her a hard look. She stared back at him, defiant and yet so sad. He wasn't sure what to think anymore, but she was right, he'd promised. "Okay, Amanda. Assuming this is all truth, how do you know about it? You work for MIB?"

"Who?"

"The Men in Black. You know, the guys from Roswell. Area 51? Alien hunters?"

"No, I don't work for MIB. They aren't real," she said with a dismissive flick of her hand. It was as if MIB were the most ludicrous thing to believe in. Jason almost laughed. After the story she'd spun MIB sounded downright sane.

Amanda turned and looked out at the ocean. It was murky, and rain-swollen, but for so many species, both terrestrial and non, water was the birthplace of life and she'd always been drawn to it.

"Jason, let me finish, please."

She didn't see him nod but continued. "Unlike Earth's amoebas you can see Acanthans with the naked eye, but only barely and they are sentient. They have a mission."

"And what would that be?"

"To infect whatever species they found."

"Of course it is," Jason said derisively.

Amanda looked over her shoulder and glared. "What

they found on the Carolina coast was a treasure trove of people who spent the hot summer months swimming in the warm water."

"Infect?"

"Yes, infect. Or perhaps finding a host body would be better."

"Host body does not sound better."

"Perhaps not, but it's more accurate." She thought briefly of all those thousands of Acanthan lost. At the mercy of the currents, some were torn apart by storms, eaten by phytoplankton; or swallowed by sea life. Less than one hundred of the nearly three thousand creatures that had survived millennia of space travel had made it to shore.

"How the hell do they find people? Chance?"

"They can track the electronic signal emitted by mammalian hearts. Any mammals that use the shallow coastal waters were targeted. They had no way of knowing so many species populate this planet."

"So not all of them found humans?"

"No. Some found their way into other animals like pets or wildlife. Only a handful made it into the bodies of humans and not all were adult humans."

"You mean kids were infected?"

"Of course. Microbes don't discriminate. They just want a viable host. Nothing more. Nothing less."

"Do I want to ask how they infect?"

"Probably not. When people are infected, they get disoriented and confused. Some might look or sound drunk."

"Like the people at work."

She turned, and Jason could see her playing with her

necklace. She absently rolled the small black stone back and forth between her fingers. It was the one he'd give her, made from the meteorite. The irony wasn't lost on him.

"Yes, like them. Unlike normal terrestrial amoeboid brain infections, we don't usually kill the host. That would be counterproductive to our purpose."

Jason stared, open mouth, at his girlfriend. "Amanda, what do you mean, 'we?'"

Amanda paled as she realized her slip.

CHAPTER THIRTEEN

Amanda could feel Jason behind her. She could feel the anger and hurt radiating from him. She couldn't blame him; she'd betrayed him, manipulated him and, as he saw it, planned on killing him. She hated herself for it. Looking back, she knew she should have acted sooner, but how do you turn on your people? No matter what she did, she'd betray someone she loved.

Amanda thought back to the first human she'd processed. She had only been Amanda for a few weeks at that point. She was cold and analytical and had found a young girl, only thirteen years old, a prodigy. Without any thought to the girl or her welfare, Amanda had drugged her and brought her to Tony for processing. It was the first time they'd tried to process a teen. It did not go well.

Amanda looked down at the girl strapped to the table. She was so young. Amanda had reservations on how well this would work. As a biologist, she understood human physiology. Children were the easiest to process with their wonderful developing brains; next were young adults whose hormone levels had evened out. The elderly were also easy to process but it was risky as they were prone to brain degradation. Teens were a different beast, filled with a cocktail of hormones that sent their brains reeling. However, Tony was insistent. The girl was impressive: a chess master by the time she was eleven, able to solve complex mathematical problems in half the time of even the most advanced computer.

Right now, she was just a scared little girl who was begging for her life. She was stripped naked, strapped to a cold metal table, and surrounded by strangers. Humans were vile to each other and Amanda knew what the girl had to be thinking. She had no way of knowing that if this worked, she'd be elevated.

Sometimes when she closed her eyes at night Amanda could still see the news flashes: "MISSING GIRL IN BOSTON AREA: JESSICA LAKE" and above it a smiling picture of Jessica with her family, her pet Jack Russell snuggled up in her arms and looking up at her adoringly. The Amanda of now wanted to cry, the Amanda from then didn't care.

Tony handed Amanda a petri dish with four small amoebas swimming in the clear fluid.

"I've decided to give her to you," Tony cooed as he ran his hands over her arms and she smiled over her shoulder at him, while Jessica sobbed on the table below them. "These are your children. Pick one, give them life."

"Are you sure? At her age this could be problematic."

"I'm sure." He looked down at the girl hungrily and she began to cry. Amanda's only response was a nod.

Jessica looked up pleadingly at Amanda. "Please, lady. Let me go. I promise I won't tell anyone," she sobbed. Amanda looked down at her coldly, analytically. Tears streaked the girl's pale face and plastered her brown hair to her face. Gently Amanda brushed the hairs aside; they'd be in the way.

"Shush, child. Everything will be okay. We have no intentions of hurting you. We're here to help."

Maybe she'd be okay, maybe they'd let her go. That small spark of hope lit her face and she gave Amanda a small tentative smile. The innocence of youth made her want to trust someone. Anyone. She knew the man, who was now standing a few feet away behind the woman, was evil. The woman might had taken her, but she'd not abused her. The creepy skinny man was the one who had stripped her and tied her down. When she struggled, he'd hit her hard, splitting her lip and swelling one eye almost shut; but maybe the woman would help?

Her brief hope was crushed as Amanda took a squishy worm from the dish and placed it in the palm of her hand, where it squirmed and wriggled. Gently she stroked it and looked at it with affection.

"This is my gift to you," Amanda said.

"What... what is that?" Jessica asked between sobs.

"This is humanity's salvation," Amanda said as she slid her offspring off her hand and onto the girls' face.

Jessica whimpered and tried to shake it free. Her head was strapped down so her movements were small and futile. The slimy little thing held fast and worked its way into her nose. She could feel it slithering its way inside. She'd been crying hard and the mucous helped the Acanthan work its way in faster. It was only a few minutes before it reached her brain. The small creature latched onto the cerebellum and small fibrous tendrils dove into Jessica's brain, wrapping around it and fighting for control.

It felt like her skull was on fire. She screamed and thrashed as the Acanthan's tentacles burrowed deep. Screams tore her throat raw. Amanda looked at Tony, "We need to find a solu-

tion to this. They make too much noise and are going to harm the host."

"Yes. Anesthesia might be a good solution."

"We'll have to see how hard it is to get a hold of."

Amanda and Tony watched dispassionately while a war of survival raged inside the girl's body, Acanthan versus Earthling. In this particular battle, neither would win. Jessica's eyes rolled up in her head as she began to convulse. Spasms wracked her body as her muscles involuntarily contracted and relaxed in rapid fire. There was a loud snap as a bone in her arm broke. Her jaw was clenched so tight she bit her tongue and bloody froth poured from her mouth. Slowly the spasms reduced to twitches which reduced to stillness.

Amanda checked for a pulse and shook her head when there was no flutter of life beneath her fingertips.

"Damn it," Tony grumbled. "She was so promising."

"I feared something like this would happen, though I confess I was not expecting this violent a reaction."

"It was unexpected."

"Teens will be difficult, their bodies are in too much of a state of chemical and hormonal flux to adapt to the symbiote. They will carry a high risk of rejection."

"Pity," Tony said as he turned to leave.

"Dispose of her, will you?"

Amanda looked down at the lifeless form.

"Of course."

Jessica's body was found three days later by a fisherman who'd taken his kids out on the Neponset River. One of his children had spotted something pale bobbing in the water near the shoreline. The police retrieved her cold, bloated body from where it had caught on a tree. The police said it was murder, but they *had no suspects. Amanda had made sure there was no link back to CloneZone or herself. She'd watched every news piece she could find on it. The girl's death bothered her. She couldn't figure out why but every time she thought about Jessica, she felt a little sick to her stomach and she wanted to cry.*

It was very un-Acanthan.

Amanda felt weak and nauseated as the memory washed over her. She'd hurt so many people. Killed people. Children. At the time she'd convinced herself that she was trying to save them, to save humanity from it's violent and self-destructive tendencies. She shook her head, but it wasn't the truth. It was a lie she'd accepted to make what she did easier. An excuse to exterminate an entire species. The truth was exactly what she'd told Jason, they were an invasion force. Their goal was to spread, take over the sentient species of the planet, make them Acanthan.

She sometimes wondered if they'd come to humanity in peace, would some humans have volunteered? Likely not. Humans were a xenophobic species and clannish to a fault, and Acanthans were obsessed with spreading. From what she knew of people, most would prefer death to any type of control.

She couldn't do anything to bring Jessica or the others that had been sacrificed back, but she could honour them by saving those that she could.

Amanda looked out over the water. She took a deep breath and closed her eyes for a moment, forcing the tears for all those gone from the corner of her eyes. The ocean soothed her, and right now she needed soothing and to be able to focus more than she ever had before.

She loved Earth's oceans; they reminded her of Acantha, though it was the wrong colour. Oceans were the birthplace of so many species throughout the universe. Even here on Earth, all life came from the sea and the variety and number were staggering, an anomaly in the universe. Most of humanity, with their myopic view of day-to-day life, didn't stop to look at the beauty that surrounded them. A few looked up, but they were rare.

Amanda considered herself an Earthling. She'd been born here and by human measurement she was only a couple of years old, but by microbial standards she was born mature with a full set of memories from all her predecessors encoded on her mitochondrial DNA. She could access them as needed. She closed her eyes as flashes of memory flicked behind her eyes.

She was swimming in the warm pink ocean that teemed with microbial life. There were only a few multi-cell life forms on the planet and only one of them sentient. The two species developed on different parts of the planet, so they knew nothing of each other until the mammals began to explore. All it took was one of the mammals swimming, and it was sheer accident that the amoeba slipped in but when it did, it took the mammal as its recipient. Instead of being hosts, the mammalian Acanthan species developed a symbiotic relationship with their tiny invaders. The microbe and mammal shared a consciousness with each other. It was this hybridization that gave the microbes mobility and true self-awareness. Together they augmented each other. The Acanthan intelligence developed exponentially and it was only a few millennia before they'd achieved space flight. Interstellar flight and conquest came shortly after. Planets that the

Acanthan body could withstand were rare so their invasion plan was simple: fill a rock with the microbes, shoot it at the planet from outside the solar system and wait. Simple and safe.

She remembered the feeling of the soft blue fur on her body, the colony ships, and generation upon generation travelling through space. Memories of being selected for colonization, being placed in the rock, years of travel in that little rock, the brutal entry through Earth's atmosphere and the shock of Earth's oceans flitted through her mind, bringing her back to the recent past.

How could she ever explain all of this to Jason? How could any human ever understand? Especially one who knew she'd been sent to get him.

"Amanda..." Tony cooed in her ear as he ran his hands over Amanda's shoulders. She fought hard to stop from pulling away as she sat in the briefing room with the two other members of the Earth-bound Acanthan leadership. Tony was her superior officer and under Acanthan law, she and all other of his subordinates were at his mercy.

"Yes, sir?"

"We've a new assignment for you. A young human named Jason Donoghue."

"Yes, he's a very promising MIT student. I found him." Walter sat there smugly. Amanda refused to acknowledge Walter's comment and, as they held equal rank, she could.

His obsequious and sycophantic attitude irritated her. He did everything he could to ingratiate himself with Tony and it worked.

Tony smiled at Walter, allowing him his moment. "A computer engineering major. He's also got a biology background. He's perfect for the position we have available. We need to finish *that project. Walter did well in finding this one," Tony said, giving Amanda a very pointed look.*

"Even though he's not in charge of recruitment."

"Very good work, Walter," Amanda said with a brief nod. It irked her to give him any credit. If she didn't acknowledge Walter, they'd know how much this did irritate her and she'd never give them that pleasure. She turned to look at Tony, who'd gone to sit across from his protégé. "Standard procedure?" she asked.

Tony shook his head. "Not with this one. He really has some of the best potential we've seen in quite some time and he is easy to get to. As you know, the less afraid a subject is when processed the better the chance of success, so we want him to be as relaxed as possible."

"Very well, sir. What would you like me to do?"

"Seduce him."

"I beg your pardon?" Amanda raised her eyebrows so high it looked like they were trying to meet her hairline. "You want me to do what?"

"You heard me. Seduce him."

"That is not in my job description."

"It is now," Walter said as he looked her up and down with a look of disgust. "You've finally gotten an assignment that you should be good at."

Amanda rounded on the older man and growled. "Shut up, you old coot."

"Commanders," Tony snapped.

Amanda and Walter turned from each other sharply and faced their Captain.

"Yes, sir," they said in unison, though Amanda still managed to glare at Walter from the corner of her eye.

"Amanda, you can see that of the three of us, you are uniquely suited to this role. An attractive young woman, slightly younger than he is. You are both interested in the sciences and have much in common. You have a chance at striking up a conversation with him that is natural and would leave him unsuspecting of any ulterior motives."

Amanda nodded as Tony continued.

"Neither I nor Walter have this in with him. He'd suspect something right from the start."

Amanda mulled it over for a while as she leafed through the small dossier they had on Jason. She held up a photo they had downloaded from MIT's database. Not bad looking at all, so this mission wouldn't be as dismal as she'd feared, and his dossier was impressive. A young software entrepreneur, he'd saved up all the money to attend school. He was only working to cover his day-to-day expenses. IQ of 155, foundation in engineering and human biology. Yes, he'd be a valuable asset if they could recruit him without any corruption. She put the photo down and looked at Tony. "Very well. When do I start?"

Tony smiled and said, "Go to the bar he works at, meet him there and work your magic."

CHAPTER FOURTEEN

Marc found himself fighting his way back to consciousness. It was like swimming to the surface after a deep dive; watery haloed lights flickered before his barely opened eyes. His arms, no, his whole body felt heavy. He lay still and listening to the sound of his breathing. There was a dull ache that thrummed through his body.

"I'm still alive."

Forcing his eyes fully open, Marc found that he was still in the same cold, dry, antiseptic room with the hospital smell, complete with the pervasive undertone of death that stuck in his throat, making him gag. Whatever they'd used to drug him must have been finally wearing off because the dizziness and disorientation were gone, thinking was easier, and his head didn't hurt so much.

Marc tried to sit but the effort was short-lived thanks to the thick leather straps that were still firmly in place. He gave a few futile angry jerks against the restraints.

"Fuck." His voice sounded hollow in the noiseless room and with a frustrated growl he let his head flop back down.

From his limited vantage point, Marc tried to look

around. Someone had been in. The room was brighter, and a soft cotton sheet had been draped over him. Slowly he looked to the right again, hoping he'd been wrong about what he'd seen the last time he had been awake. No, he hadn't been mistaken, George was still dead. Whomever had killed him hadn't even bothered to cover the body. He was horrible to look at; his flesh was a pale grey and flaccid, with the purple bruising from lividity just beginning to show along the backs of his arms and legs.

Gulping the fetid air to try and keep from vomiting on himself, Marc looked back up at the ceiling and closed his eyes. Bile rose in his throat, burning. He suspected that puking in his current predicament wouldn't be pleasant.

He was afraid to look and see what had befallen Jamie while he'd slept. Would he see her cold and lifeless body, with creamy blue-white eyes staring into nothing? As soon as he was sure he had control of his stomach, he turned his head.

Jamie was alive and looking perfectly healthy. Her restraints had been removed, and she was sitting cross-legged on the gurney, dressed in a simple blue hospital gown with a blanket laid across her lap. She was holding her hands in front of her and was playing with her fingers. She was looking at them in awe, as if she'd never seen them before. She had a huge smile, and her red hair was hanging limply around her face.

He tried to speak but his voice was little more than a croak. He worked his mouth to summon a little moisture and managed a hoarse whisper. "Jamie, thank God you're alive."

She didn't respond. "What the hell?" His thoughts

were quickly going from relief to surprise at seeing her free then to hurt and anger. "If she's free, why hasn't she bothered to try and help me?"

"Jamie? Jamie, you okay? Can you help me? Do you know where we are?"

Jamie didn't so much as turn her head but replied, "Why yes, Mother, I'd love some ice cream," and then began to pantomime eating a bowl of ice cream. Jamie should be freaking out about being in a locked room, but she sat there calmly eating her invisible ice cream.

"Shit," he said, letting his head flop down. He gave the room another look, as best he could from his awkward position. It wasn't overly large, only twenty feet square with blank white seamless walls and a ten-foot-high ceiling. The only lighting came from the pot lights spaced evenly about the ceiling. Only half of the lights worked and of the ones that did, most were flickering, giving the room a surreal strobing effect. Against the far wall he could just make out the outline of some cabinets and a sink, but his position prevented him from seeing the wall behind his head or the floor below. Lined up side by side in the middle of the room were four narrow wheeled gurneys with sides that could be raised. He, George, and Jamie occupied three; one was vacant. All the gurneys were adorned with the brown leather restraining straps and each gurney had its own instrument trays filled with bizarre looking tools and dishes.

"Fuck," Marc muttered again while giving another tug on his restraints. He didn't like feeling helpless. "We've gotta get the fuck outta here."

He was talking out loud to Jamie. He'd figured out she

wasn't here mentally and probably wouldn't respond but talking out loud helped calm him. And he needed that right now: calm and focus. It was up to him to find a way out.

With deliberate actions he began to test his bonds. All three straps were still in place, but the hip strap was just a little looser. He didn't know if it was from all his wiggling or if it was someone's error. Either way, he wasn't going to waste this opportunity.

With some effort he managed to wriggle his right arm up until his elbow was bent at a very uncomfortable angle. His attempts were halted when his wrist brought up against the strap.

"No freaking way." Marc gritted his teeth and twisted his wrist, dragging it hard against the rough leather. Friction burned his skin and tore flesh. He bit down on his lip to stop himself from crying out. Blood smeared over his wrist, wetting the leather and lubricating the strap. With one final tug he pulled his lower arm free and then did the same with his other arm, but now he felt a little like a T-Rex. He could move and wave his arms from the elbows down but couldn't reach anything.

Blindly he felt around. He ran his hands over the leather chest strap but could not feel anything that might be a fastener. He moved on to the one on his hips. As he felt along, he touched cool metal. He lifted his head to try and see but the buckle was too low down on his left hip. It was a simple thick leather strap with a belt buckle fastener. He tried to pull it free, but it was too tight, and he was one-handed.

Taking a deep breath, Marc tried to relax his body as

much as he could, hoping it would release the tension on the strap. His fingers barely reached, and he painstakingly worked the leather through the buckle. It felt like it took forever, but he finally heard a soft clink as the strap fell free.

This freedom gave him some wiggle room. Using the sides of the gurney as leverage, Marc grasped them and began wiggling and squirming. Slowly, he managed to work himself down the table until his shoulders and arms were completely free. The pressure from the leg strap bit into his bare flesh. Determined, Marc ignored it and pushed on.

The top strap was still high around his neck when he ran out of room to scrunch down, but by then his arms were free and he was able to quickly undo that strap. The moment he was unfettered, Marc sat up. A wave of dizziness washed over him, and he gripped the sides of the gurney for balance.

"Too fast," he said and shook his head while taking slow deep breaths. He took a quick look at Jamie who was still sitting there examining the fine details of her fingers.

Once he was steadied, Marc quickly undid the final restraint. As it fell away, he stretched his muscles, feeling the cramping and stiffness. He must have been out for a couple of hours at least.

Finally, he stood. The floor was icy beneath his feet and with a start he realized that he was still naked. Shooting a bashful glance at Jamie, his normally olive complexion flushed a deep crimson. Someone, a stranger, had completely undressed him. There was a stack of gowns like the one Jamie was wearing on the counter behind where he'd been lying. He reached over and grabbed one, pulling it on quickly and tying the straps behind his back.

He felt violated. A shudder of revulsion ran down his spine as he thought about how completely helpless he'd been. He had no memory of anything after the classroom. What had they done to him? As he looked over at Jamie, who had gone back to eating her invisible ice cream, and George's lifeless form, Marc reached behind him to pull the gown closed over his rear end and wondered if he would even remember if anything had been done to him.

Or if he wanted to.

CHAPTER FIFTEEN

Amanda had done as she was instructed. Her job was to recruit; she was good at it and she knew that Jason wouldn't stand a chance. People trusted the perky young woman with the wide earnest smile. She'd recruited scientists, business people, politicians, grandparents. She'd tricked them all saying she was a student looking to do a work term or doing a report. No one suspected. Humans were gross and violent. They took pleasure in killing other species, even their own. What Amanda hadn't counted on was falling in love. Real, human emotional love. Acanthans fancied themselves logical. They did have feelings; however logic would dictate their course of action. Emotions were frowned upon as motivational forces.

Bonding with humans changed this factor. Their complex mix of hormones and neurochemicals associated with these emotions overwhelmed the Acanthans. It affected them all: in Tony it presented as becoming addicted to personal pleasures, mostly food and sex, while Walter was hooked on daytime and reality television, and Amanda, well, she'd fallen in love with her assignment.

A smile flicked at the corner of her lips as she remembered the first time she saw Jason. He was behind the bar in that dingy dive, wiping everything down as he went and laughing with the patrons. The place stank and it took all she had to not turn on her heel and leave. Especially after the bar's patrons started ogling her as she walked across the floor and climbed up onto a bar stool. Then Jason turned to her, smiled, and she'd looked into his bright green eyes as he said, "What can I getcha?" In that moment she had felt something. Something she'd never felt before: raw physical attraction. The part of her that was Amanda recognized it—she'd felt it before—but her Acanthan part flinched. This was not part of the plan. Gamely she tried to stay focused that night, but as they'd talked, she felt more at ease with him. It was almost as if they'd known each other for years as they'd talked about none-sense, a word she used when humans made small talk about nothing important, none-sense. It was foolish talk about school, the wacky weather, videogames, favourite moves, books, you name it and they probably touched on it that night. She'd had fun and she wasn't sure what to do about it.

Over the months she worked on building a rapport with Jason, convincing him to give up his night job and go to work at CloneZone. He didn't want to, but she'd told him how important it was that he have a regular job with regular hours. She'd convinced him that MIT would still be there waiting for him.

Tony and Walter were thrilled at her progress. They were going to get the computer engineer they so desperately needed. Tony was so anxious he wanted to process Jason on his first week at CloneZone, but Jason skipped work that day, calling in that he had a last-minute appointment. Next time he was stuck on a call. Then he'd been late. Every time they'd set up for a new class to process, Jason wasn't there. Amanda had helped by changing class time, but she'd been unable to do it all. Tony himself had set up some of the classes, but still Jason dodged the bullet. If she'd been religious, it was almost as if divine intervention were interceding on his behalf. Tony was getting impatient. He wanted Jason processed and working on the code they needed.

She shook her head and droplets of icy water spattered across her face. She'd grown to care for Jason and by extension humanity. Watching her co-workers, people she'd befriended, wander around bumping into walls, the blood curdling screams from those who had awakened during the process, and disposing of the bodies of men and women that didn't survive had eroded her Acanthan dispassion. Amanda's empathy grew with each person she helped process, and it became harder and harder for her to send someone to the grinder. She was trapped. Tony would kill her rather than see her defect or even if he suspected how *human* she'd become.

Even before Jason she had stopped being in the centre when a processing was happening. She'd found herself falsifying candidate information to make them less appealing or harder to find, she'd delayed adding people to training and she'd purposefully ordered scented nitrous oxide gas, hoping that the smell would alert the victims to their peril. The scented gas had worked, people had fled the room, and when it couldn't be explained by the manager, they left.

"Why the fuck did you order that shit? We lost three

classes of hosts yesterday," Tony had yelled at her as he paced back and forth their staging room.

"You try finding a place that will deliver nitrous oxide gas to a printing company without asking any questions," she snapped back. "I had to get it from the black market. It wasn't easy or cheap and it was the only stuff available. If it's not satisfactory, you can do your own ordering."

She normally felt safe to speak to him this way when Walter wasn't around. Tony was her commanding officer but also her Acanthan parent. She'd misjudged his anger.

"Do you want to get written up for insubordination?" he hissed through clenched teeth.

Amanda looked at Tony in shock.

She'd never seen him this angry with her. Insubordination to an officer of Tony's rank was a capital offence. Punishment could mean removal from the host or worse. Did he suspect her?

"No, sir," she said meekly.

"Order more. Until then I'll get Walter to have the locks rigged to set automatically. That should solve our problem for now."

Still, she'd managed to slow things down and save a few people. It wasn't much, but it was a start. Then she'd met Jason. Initially she'd planned on finding a way to convince Tony that this kid wasn't worth the effort, that the dossier was wrong.

Today she realized just how much she really did love him. The reality had scared her.

Tony was printing off papers and grinning from ear to ear.

"Why are you so happy?"

"Your idiot boyfriend just gave me the chance I've been waiting for."

"What do you mean?"

"He was late. I put him on probation with required training. Training that you will schedule for today." Tony tapped his little stack off papers to the tune of shave and a haircut. "I am finally going to get him into that classroom."

"I hear a *but* in there."

"You certainly do. He called me a, what was it now?" Tony put his finger to his lips as he tried to recall precisely the name Jason called him. "Oh, that's right. He called me a 'Goddamned troll fucker.'" "To your face?"

"No. He didn't have the balls for that.

I heard him mumble it as he walked away."

Amanda tried to stifle her laugh. It came out as a snort.

"Do you find something amusing, Commander?" Tony said as he tried to puff himself up.

"He looks like an overstuffed chicken," Amanda thought to herself, fighting back more laughter.

"No, Captain. Please continue. What is your plan now?"

Tony smiled and it scared Amanda. "Oh Amanda, we are going to process him, but I'm using the next gens."

"Tony, you can't."

His head snapped up and a frown pulled his narrow lips down into a thin line. "You forget yourself. I can and I will." He gave her a long hard stare. "If I didn't know better, I'd say you were concerned."

Amanda drew herself up. "You misunderstand me.

He's a valuable asset and they aren't ready. He'll go mad."

He nodded, "I've supplied Walter with a syringe filled with ketamine."

"Animal tranquilizer? Why?"

"If he goes mad during processing, we will deal with him. Permanently."

"Oh," Amanda said as she chewed on her bottom lip.

Tony was taken aback. "You do not approve?" he said sharply.

Amanda looked up quickly. "I was just thinking..." Amanda's thoughts trailed off as she tried to come up with some reason for her concerns.

"But?"

"As I already said, he's a valuable resource. I thought we were going to make the most of him. "

"That would be preferable but at this point I'll take what I can get."

"Let me look into it, see what I can come up with. Maybe we can increase the odds of his survival."

Tony waved her off with dismissive flick of his hand. "Do whatever you feel is necessary. Just ensure there is a nice, compliant and processed Jason waiting for me after work."

With a nod, she turned on her heel and left. She didn't want Jason processed, didn't want him to change, and certainly didn't want him dead. She liked the Jason she had, but she had no idea what she was going to do between now and the afternoon to change things or get him out once and for all. Not without getting them both killed.

CHAPTER SIXTEEN

Amanda felt her world spin around her.

"Amanda. Answer me," Jason insisted.

Amanda couldn't look at Jason, couldn't speak. The words were stopped by the lump in her throat. She shook her head.

"Damn it, Amanda, don't dare you leave it there. Are you one of them?" Jason's voice was bitter and angry.

After what felt like an eternity, Amanda said weakly, "I meant they." For the first time in her existence Amanda was ashamed of what she was.

"Like hell you did." Jason wanted to throw up. "The truth. Now." Jason was desperate to know. "Or I'll go ask Tony."

With a sob she blurted out, "Yes, it's *we*." Once the words started, she couldn't stop them. "Me, Tony, Walter, all of upper management, the entire crew of the printing centre and by now most of the call centre."

"Fuck. Me." Jason felt weak. "So, you're saying I'm working for fucking brain-eating aliens?"

Amanda nodded as tears streamed down her face. She hated this human body sometimes and its weaknesses.

Acanthans were creatures of logic, humans were nothing more than balls of emotion in a meat wrapping.

"I swear if I close my eyes, I'll hear Rod Serling." Jason paused to take a deep, steadying breath before continuing. "Where are Scully and Mulder when you need them?"

"Who?" Amanda asked.

Jason just looked at her and wondered how he'd ever fallen for her. It had to be some alien pheromone bullshittery. She/it/Amanda didn't know who Serling or Mulder were. "Assuming I believe this, is any of the real Amanda left?"

"Yes. I am Amanda."

"Bullshit. Pretty sure Amanda's real brain wasn't made up of cytoplasm."

"Her current brain isn't made up of cytoplasm. I guess it's really, *we* are Amanda. We don't erase the person. Not completely. We bond with them. Through the bond we get access to most of their memories and feelings. Once we're, well, attached, their thoughts become ours; ours, become theirs. We literally become them outside of some insignificant memory loss, . So really, no one has died."

"That is only a technicality." Anger flushed his face.

"An important one."

"So, you're a parasite and *my* Amanda is gone."

It was Amanda's turn to be angry. "We aren't a parasite. We're intelligent and she was never *your* Amanda. You didn't own her. Furthermore, you never met her. You've only ever known me."

Jason reeled backwards. "Wait. What?" he asked, dumbstruck.

"That's right. Me. You fell in love with a, as you put

it, *brain-eating alien*." She said the words with such venom and self-hatred Jason almost felt bad for her. Amanda saw her chance to finally drive Jason away. "The only reason we met was because Tony wanted to recruit you. I was *sent* to you. I was your recruitment officer."

"What the hell do you mean?" Jason looked as if he'd been slapped. All colour had drained from his face and he looked sick.

"I mean, the hierarchy wanted you. We've been re-cruiting highly intelligent people with specific skills. Any one of those jobs would have put you in a great position as one of our agents. They wanted you badly. A nice young, hormone-driven human male. Ripe for the picking."

She turned to look at him. She pulled the shield of Acanthan arrogance and superiority around herself. She stood tall, looking down her nose at him, even though he was taller than her. He was staring at her slack-jawed. Each word struck home like a knife. "So, we studied you and knew you'd respond to a pretty face. We groomed you. It was the long way of getting you in position, but it worked." She smiled evilly. "Processing is so much more effective when the host is receptive."

"So, I was nothing more than your assignment."

Amanda didn't answer his question. She couldn't. "You have a wonderful mind. We wanted it."

"You can't have it," Jason growled.

"I know that now. You'd have been processed by now if you hadn't missed every single training session. Tony was ready to cut you from the program. Take the loss. I thought you had too much potential, so I convinced him and scheduled you in one last time."

"The training session this afternoon." It was a statement, not a question.

"Yes."

"What would have happened if I'd gone?"

"You'd have been processed." Her voice was dead, void of any emotion.

Jason waited, letting her words sort themselves out in his reeling mind. He felt angry, confused, hurt, and scared all at the same time. Each emotion took centre stage for a brief, painful moment before being shoved out of the way by the next in a flickering emotional kaleidoscope. His head spun, and his stomach heaved as he sat down heavily on the wharf. He was shivering with a mix of cold and shock.

"Aliens?" he thought. "Fucking aliens."

He looked over at Amanda. She looked like a half-drowned rat. Her blonde hair was dirty and plastered to her head and face. Her wet clothes clung to her. He wanted to feel sorry for her, a small part already did, but he couldn't. She had this look about her. She looked like Amanda, but not the one he'd known. When she looked at him, he felt like a bug. As he looked at her, anger won out, pushing all the other emotions aside. She was a bug, but she considered him nothing more than a host to be taken. He was a meat suit. He shook his head and as he did some pieces of Amanda's story began to click together. He looked up sharply at her and demanded, "Where's Marc?"

Amanda was caught off guard and answered, "Training."

"You mean, processed." His words came out through

teeth clenched in anger.

"Oh," she whispered, looking away again. "He'll be a host by now."

"Fuck," Jason yelled. "Fuck everything." He kicked a thick wooden pier piling, sending a shot of pain up his foot and ankle. He barely noticed it. He was angry. Angrier than he'd ever been. He was fighting back rage as he turned towards Amanda and she stepped back, her eyes wide. She'd never been afraid of Jason, but he seemed on the verge of completely losing it.

"Jason?" she said, a quaver in her voice.

He saw her look of fear and in this moment he didn't care. Something inside him had snapped when he'd realized he and his best friend had been betrayed by the woman he loved. "I'm going back."

"No."

"I'm not asking you for permission," he said flatly. He looked at her. He didn't even really know her, but he knew he couldn't save Marc by himself. Grinding his teeth as he spoke, Jason said, "As much as I don't want to, I'm asking for your help."

"Jason, I…" Amanda hesitated.

"No more, Amanda. You've told me repeatedly that you got me out today because you love me. "

"I do." Amanda stepped forward, hope in her eyes. Jason stepped back from her; the look of anger and disgust stopped her in her tracks.

"You have to choose. Now."

"Jason, please don't–"

He cut her off abruptly. "No. Enough. I'm not a fool. You've told me enough that I can guess some of what you've done. Now you can begin trying to make up for some of it. Help me save Marc."

Amanda hung her head. Jason had no idea that she'd been subverting Tony's plans for months. That she'd nearly been caught a dozen times or more, often only being saved by the fact that it was inconceivable than an Acanthan would turn against their own. Her chest felt tight. "Jason, I..." she again began to plead.

"Your next words better be 'I'll help.'" His face was hard, and his hands were clenched in white-knuckled fists by his sides.

Amanda sighed and dropped her shoulders in defeat. "I'll help."

A wave of relief washed over Jason and she could see him visibly relax.

"We need a plan," he said.

"If Walter sees you, he will alert Tony right away."

"I know. Is there a back entrance we can use?"

Amanda nodded as she turned to look back out over the water. "I can distract Walter, tell him I lost my ID, so he has to come let me in. You can use my ID to get in through the side door."

"Walter saw us run out. It was obvious I was chasing you. Even he's not stupid enough to let that go, especially when he sees your ID check pop up on his computer when I use it to get in." Frustrated, Jason scrubbed his hands through his damp hair.

"The only way you are going to get in unnoticed is to use the side exit."

"You go on in. You can tell him some stupid excuse about us having a fight. I'll go around to the side exit and once you get past Walter you can let me in through there."

Turning to look at Jason, Amanda nodded her assent. "Okay."

They walked in silence back to the building, Amanda running the past couple of hours over in her head, Jason thinking of nothing more than trying to save his friend.

"Shit," he said as he stopped abruptly, putting his hand on Amanda's arm.

"What's wrong?"

Jason pointed to a large boxy white security camera on the wall angled so that it was pointing down at the front door. "We forgot about the security cameras."

"Damn it."

CHAPTER SEVENTEEN

Marc was hungry, cold, and really pissed off. He scanned the walls looking for a doorway, but they looked seamless. There had to be a door. They weren't transported into a sealed room, that only existed in science fiction.

"Who or what would want to kidnap a bunch of call centre agents?" he said out loud. "And why?" His voice echoed back to him.

He couldn't think of anyone who would want to kidnap the three of them. He tried to think of any link. They didn't have any money and the company sure wouldn't pay to get them back. Call centre agents were eminently replaceable. Their families weren't wealthy. None of them were exceptional. Sure, they all had degrees, but in different fields; George had sociology, Jamie had done environmental science, and Marc had done meteorology.

So, they were all intelligent and well educated, which wasn't unusual in this business, but who kidnaps people just because they are smart? A memory from history class flitted through his mind: Nazis. Nazis kidnapped smart people and forced them to develop weapons. Marc shook his head at the ludicrousness of the thought; this was 21st century America, not Nazi Germany. Nothing like that could happen here.

A more likely culprit would be a psycho. But how would they target three random people or be able to boobytrap a classroom to capture them, let alone drag the bodies out of the building?

"Not helpful," he said to himself. His musings wouldn't get them out of there.

"Focus, you idiot. What do you think, Jamie?"

"Buttercups."

"Exactly. First order of business, I need pants." Pants, boxers, anything would do. He felt vulnerable with his freezing bits hanging out. A quick search of the cabinets resulted in some paper surgical pants, which he quickly pulled on under the gown. They crinkled and made swooshing noises when he walked, but at least his backside, and more importantly his front side, wasn't hanging out anymore.

He quickly went through the remaining cabinets, hoping to find something, anything, that would help get him out. They were filled with basic hospital supplies: boxes of gloves and masks, stacks of gowns, trays of forceps, something that reminded Marc of the speculums he'd seen when his wife was having their son, only much smaller.

"What the hell are those for?"

His imagination filled in that blank spot and sent a shudder down his spine. Quickly he moved on. There were syringes and a few scalpels. One cabinet was filled with vials of something called Ketamine HCL injection. There was something familiar about the name, but Marc couldn't recall it. He brushed the thought aside as he spotted a large brown box labelled "IV Needles," which still had the invoice attached.

"Hey, Jamie, this might have an address or give an idea of where we are."

Jamie only giggled. His heart racing, Marc reached for the box; the ink had faded on the form. He tore the sheet off the box and stepped under a light to read it. The needles had been ordered from a medical supplier in Chicago. An icy chill washed over him as he read the receiving address.

"What in the ever-loving fuck would CloneZone need IV needles for?" Marc asked of a non-responsive Jamie.

He looked at the signing name. "Amanda Blue?" Jason's Amanda? Marc's stomach twisted. What the hell was going on?

"Amanda. Amanda knew about this?" he said out loud.

Jamie replied, "Manda?"

Marc looked at her hopefully. She was still as vacant as earlier; she was just parroting him.

"What the hell is going on here?' he thought. Was CloneZone a human trafficking front? Working for the government doing secret experiments? Each idea was outlandish and even as he thought of them, he felt foolish.

As crazy as it seemed, there was something illicit going on. The classroom was rigged with knockout gas and he was standing in what was a moderately well-stocked medical facility. Looking from George's cold body to Jamie's crazed countenance he wondered again what had been done to them. He wondered what had been done to him. With a laugh that bordered mania, Marc cycled back to his earlier thought. Had aliens invaded? While he had missing time, he still felt normal, and he didn't have any weird memories of scientists, little grey men, or anal probing.

"Next I'll be buying tinfoil in bulk."

"Foil," Jamie agreed, giggling.

Panic and dread threatened to overwhelm him.

"Jamie, we've got to get the hell outta here. They got us in here, so there has to be an exit somewhere." Looking around the blank walls he couldn't easily see where a door might be.

"Chickens," Jamie said gleefully.

CHAPTER EIGHTEEN

They stayed well back, hiding behind the cars in the parking lot. The rain began to fall once more. Amanda's brow furrowed and she nibbled her bottom lip as she stared at the security camera. Jason saw her, it was something she often did when she was thinking, and he had always thought it cute. The unwelcome surge of affection for her angered him and he pushed the feelings aside. "She's an alien, you idiot," he thought.

Amanda turned and, for the first time since their argument, looked directly into Jason's eyes. She tried to ignore her stomach twisting at the look of revulsion on his face.

"Jason, you're determined to do this?"

"Yes, even if I have to go through Walter to get inside."

With a resigned sigh she continued.

"I've got an idea. But it's really risky."

"Shoot."

"See the smoke shack?"

The "smoke shack" was a semi-sheltered pergola where the office's resident smokers would go for their breaks and was currently occupied by five people, all huddled together like penguins in the middle. Puffs of grey and white smoke wafted up from the collective.

"Where are you going with this?" he asked.

"Tailgate them."

"What? They'll see me."

Amanda squinted to see who was under the pergola. Even with her augmented sight it was hard to see details between the wooden slats that surrounded the exterior.

"I'm pretty sure only one of them is processed." She glanced up at the sky, squinting as raindrops hit her face. "For once this rain will work to our advantage. Just keep your hoodie up and head down. When they head back in slip in behind them. Keep your card in your hand for show, but don't let it go near the sensor. You can follow them right in."

"Risky."

"I told you it was." She paused and looked at the doors, only a few hundred feet away. "I'll go in ahead and keep Walter busy. Once you are inside, go right, then down the hallway that leads to the emergency exit and wait for me there."

Jason looked at the group huddled in the small shelter. "We'll have to time this perfectly."

"We're probably going to get killed," Amanda said.

Jason nodded, his face set and determined. "Do you have any other suggestions?"

"Notify the authorities?"

Jason let out a quiet snort. "They'd have us committed. 'Officer, aliens have taken over CloneZone and they are about to stick a slug in my best friends' brain.'" He looked at Amanda. "It sounds insane. Without proof, all we'd do is give the cops a good hard laugh."

Amanda looked away but said nothing else.

"If we're going to do this, let's do it," Jason said and he went to step forward when Amanda stopped him with a gentle touch on his arm. He turned back to look at her. She was looking up at him with large doe eyes.

"Jason, promise me that if I don't show up in ten or fifteen minutes, you'll forget this plan and leave."

"Amanda, I can't…"

"Stop," she said in a commanding parade officer tone that brooked no argument from those on its receiving end. For the first time he could see the officer she said she was.

"You have to promise me. If I don't show up, it means Walter and Tony know, and I'm either dead or will be soon enough. You'll never find Marc without me."

Jason's heart lurched when she said "dead" with such finality. He did not want to feel anything for her.

"If you don't promise me, I'm not going in. You won't save Marc, but you can save everyone else. Leave and tell the world we exist." She paused and drew a deep breath. "There's a USB drive in our apartment. Taped to the bottom of the blue vase that I never use. It has video of processings and other proof of our tampering with the weather and communication systems."

Jason was taken aback by her confession. "Why?"

Amanda turned from him and shook her head. "There is not time for that explanation right now. Just promise me before I lose my nerve."

Reluctantly Jason said, "Fine."

"Say it."

"I promise."

Without another word, Jason headed towards the little shelter but his steps faltered when he heard her say, "Be careful. I do love you." He recovered quickly and continued without responding.

Amanda was hurt when Jason didn't respond with even a "You be careful too." She wasn't surprised and didn't blame him, but her heart still broke because he was so cold. There were times that these human emotions were so troublesome to navigate.

With a soul-weary sigh, she headed to the building, collecting herself on the way. By the time she reached the doors and shoved them open brusquely, she was a full Acanthan Commander, shoulders back and spine erect, a look of disdain fixed rigidly on her face. Walter was perched at his usual station, eyes glued to the TV screen until the door chime sounded and Amanda entered the foyer.

"Walter." She nodded as she went to walk past him. She knew he wouldn't let her go in without questioning her earlier behaviour. They were of equal rank, but he never seemed to acknowledge that fact. His age and being Tony's lackey gave him a false sense of seniority.

"You're wet," Walter said, stating the obvious. "Where have you been?"

"I've been outside and it's raining. Humans get wet when it rains."

Walter scowled at her. "Tony's been looking for you. It seems that your boyfriend disappeared from work and missed another training session."

"Not that it's any of your concern, but we had a

fight."

"So, he left work?"

"Walter, let's cut the bullshit," Amanda said with a sigh as she walked up to the counter, positioning herself so she was facing the door, and leaned over the counter to peer down at the older man. He stood to face her, making her look up at him. She scowled in distaste, but his back was to the door and that's all Amanda wanted.

"I know you saw us both run out of here."

Feeling a little more confident in this position, he crossed his arms across his chest and nodded. "Yes, I did. Why?"

Amanda could see the small herd of humans, their break finished, making a run for the door to escape the heavy rain. All of them had their hoods up and were hunched over.

Amanda looked into Walter's watery pale eyes and smiled. Helping Jason had given her one small gift she hadn't considered; she no longer had to disguise who she was. She decided it would be the perfect distraction. "Quite honestly, Walter, it's none of your goddamned business."

His puffy face went florid.

The scanner beeped once as the first person swiped in and pushed open the door to get out of the pouring rain.

"How dare you speak to me that way," Walter growled under his breath. As angry as he was, he had to keep up the pretense of being a security guard.

Beep went the scanner as the second person came through the doors held open by the first.

Amanda thought the pompous old bastard might

have a stroke and the thought gave her great pleasure. "I dare because it's about time you realized that we are the same damned rank."

The first two who had entered looked up at her comments. The first looked shocked. "Yep, Acanthan," Amanda thought. The second in line just looked confused as he held the door for person number three. Beep.

"I'm going to... I'll report... You'll be..." Walter sputtered.

Beep. Four.

"You will do exactly nothing,"

Amanda hissed at him. "Do you really want Tony to find out your particular human fetish?"

Now Walter paled to a pleasurable chalky white. "You can't know..."

Beep. Five. Amanda's heart beat faster.

"Oh, I know, and I have proof, you pompous, self serving old goat."

No beep but number six stepped through the door nodding thanks to number five as he let the door slide shut behind him. Just a few more seconds. That's all she had to buy as the smokers started to parade through the inner door.

Walter's mouth was working but no sound would come out.

"I've got all I need to bring to Tony, unless you choose to be accommodating."

After a few seconds he managed, "What do you want?"

"Any new recruits you find, you will tell me about them instead of Tony. Let one get through, and some papers will mysteriously be delivered to Tony. You will defer to me from now on."

"You bitch," Walter grumbled under his breath.

Her smile widened at the attempted insult as she watched the inner door shut behind Jason's back.

"You have no idea," she said. "Do we have an agreement?"

"Do I have a choice?"

"Of course, you do. You can choose to do as I ask or not and throw yourself on Tony's well-known mercy."

He looked apoplectic. "Yes."

"Yes what?" she said smugly.

Walter spoke through gritted teeth. "Yes, Ma'am."

Amanda nodded as she walked away from Walter, who was purple with rage.

"Now, that's better."

She pushed open the doors that led to the service hallway and with a sigh of relief collapsed against them as they closed. She looked down and saw wet footprints fading off into the distance.

"Jason," she whispered to herself and pushed off from the closed doors and headed down the hallway to the emergency exit.

Her heart skipped a beat when she saw him. He was standing just down from the security doors in a shallow alcove. He had his back turned to her and was looking down the other end of the hall. She wanted nothing more than to run to him and put her arms around him. Instead, she walked over quietly and touched his arm.

"Jason?" she said.

"Jesus Christ," Jason whisper-yelped as he jumped

and spun to face her, his arms flapping. "Christ, Amanda. Don't do that. You nearly killed me."

Amanda wanted to laugh and tried to stifle it as she replied, "I'm sorry. I didn't mean to scare you."

Jason grabbed her arm and pulled her into the alcove, looking back down the hallway where he'd been staring. "Quiet. I saw someone down there a few minutes ago. I thought it was Tony."

Amanda frowned. "Tony shouldn't be here. He should be in the processing lab with..." Amanda let her words trail off as Jason turned, looking at her with a mix of sadness and revulsion.

"I'm sorry–"

"Marc. We focus on Marc," Jason said brusquely.

She only nodded and looked at his dripping clothes. Jason was starting to shiver, as was she.

"We need to find some dry clothes. We'll stand out too much walking around sopping wet."

He looked at her quizzically. "How do you propose we do that?"

"That's easy. I'll check the lost and found," she replied with a smile.

The lost and found was a rubber tub just outside the cafeteria, located just down the hallway from Tony's cubicle office. There was a year's worth of unclaimed items sitting there waiting to be pillaged.

"You stay here. I'll just be a few minutes." Jason saw her turn to go.

"Amanda?"

"Yeah?"

"Be careful..."

Amanda smiled when he said this, but Jason didn't see, he'd turned back to watch down the other end of the hall.

"I need you to save Marc."

The smile slid from her face. She turned without another word and headed to the lunch room, past the double doors and out onto the production floor again. Technically the office was closed now, so there should not be many people around. Most would be gone home except for stragglers who had been stuck on calls or working overtime. Everyone who usually stayed after normal work hours would be in the warehouse and already processed. "Better safe than sorry," Amanda thought as she pulled off her stilettos and, barefoot, slipped past the empty cubicles until she reached the corner. She peeked around to make sure neither Tony nor Walter was hanging around Tony's desk. An empty corridor greeted her. She heaved a sigh of relief and headed the final few feet to the lunch room door.

She spotted the big green bin filled with odds and ends just inside the open archway to the open room. One wall held a counter with a couple of microwaves in cubbies. There was a fridge and a coffee machine. A grimy window was flanked by vending machines and there were tables and chairs scattered throughout in no particular pattern. It was also vacant. Amanda slipped inside and began rummaging.

It didn't take her long to find suitable dry clothes: some jeans, a worn grey t-shirt with a zombie on it that said "Beauty and Braaaaaaiiinns," and a worn looking flannel shirt that looked like they'd fit Jason. Next a pair of mismatched sneakers that were luckily in Jason's size. "Dammit," she muttered. None of the pants were women's. She grabbed a pair of grey track pants that had an elastic waist that she thought would fit her, a t-shirt with the Rolling Stones logo on the front and a pair of ugly rainbow canvas pull-on sneakers that looked to be her size. She rolled everything into a ball and stood to bring the items back to Jason.

"Amanda, my dear. Why on earth are you digging through that nasty box of leavings?"

Amanda jumped and squealed, dropping her findings back into the bin.

"Tony." She gasped. "You nearly gave me a heart attack." She had her hand over her heart and could feel it pounding against her ribs.

Tony's face creased into something that on anyone else could be taken for concern. No one who knew Tony would assume that; it was just his front. "You look pale. Are you feeling well?"

"I'm fine, sir," Amanda said, straightening herself and standing tall. She could not appear weak in front of him. "I'm just a little cold. I got caught in the downpour."

"Why were you outside?"

"Jason."

"What about him?"

"You'll have noticed by now that he wasn't in the classroom."

"Yes. His absence was disappointing." He casually took a step closer. "Especially after you promised me he'd be there."

"We got into a fight."

"Hmmm. Walter told me he saw you both running out. That was just about the time Jason should have been coming to class."

"Walter is a senile old goat."

"Amanda..." Tony said in warning.

Amanda tensed. "Fine. Jason and I got into a fight. I left and he followed me. I didn't think he'd do something like that."

Amanda paused until Tony waggled his fingers, indicating she should continue. "We fought some more, then he left. I'm heading home now. I'll take a syringe of the ketamine and sedate him there. Once he's out I'll bring him in. I'm afraid that will be the best I can do."

"Oh, Amanda, that is disappointing." Tony pouted and took another step closer and sighed dramatically. "I suppose it will have to do." His eyes flicked down to the pile of clothes she'd been holding then back up to her face. "You never did answer my question. What are you doing digging through that pile of disgusting human cast-offs?" His nose wrinkled in revulsion as he spoke.

Amanda drew herself up to her full height. Even as petite as she was, she had a presence. Her eyes flashed in irritation, and, unwittingly, Tony took a half step back from her. "Obviously I was looking for something."

"Did you find it?"

"No. You interrupted me."

"Whatever could be so interesting in there?" he said, poking the bin with his toe.

Amanda thought frantically. What could she be digging in the lost and found for? As she thought her arm brushed against her pocket.

"I've misplaced my cell. I was hoping someone dropped it in there."

"How dreadful. Nothing important on there I hope?"

"No. I don't think so anyway. It was just my personal cell." She shrugged, "Still, I wouldn't want it to be found by just anyone. Just in case."

He glanced back down at the bin, wrinkling his nose once more, and then back up to her. "Agreed. Now is not the time I want our secret to be discovered. You'd better find it." He thought for a moment, "Check with Walter, he may have found it or had it handed in."

"I'll do that," Amanda said, with a smile. She began to relax a little as Tony turned to leave. Abruptly he stopped, turned back, and stepped in close and whispered in her ear before turning on his heel and leaving without another look back.

Amanda paled and her eyes widened but said nothing her breath was caught in her throat. She just gave a curt nod. Tony smiled and left her by the bin, walking down the aisle with a cocky step.

Amanda swallowed hard. "Fuck."

CHAPTER NINETEEN

"Jamie, what do you think would work as a weapon?"

"Ice cream."

"That won't work very well," Marc thought as he searched the cupboards for something that he could use to defend himself if whomever had kidnapped them came back. He had no intentions of ending up like George. He'd seen a box labelled scalpels in one of the cupboards. He grabbed it and pulled it open; it was empty. There was nothing else of any real use in the cabinets. Looking around the room his eyes came to rest on the trays. On Jamie's tray he discovered what looked like huge six-inch tweezers, something that he could only describe as a probe, and a petri dish that held a clear liquid with slightly gelatinous blobs floating in it.

"Well, goopy jelly isn't going to help," he said as his stomach growled.

He realized it had been a long time since lunch.

"Jelly," Jamie cried.

Looking back at the petri dish he muttered as his stomach growled once again, "Mmmm, jelly."

He shook his head and walked over to the tray that had been near his gurney. "Nope, not worth it." He thought. This tray held a more promising array of tools. It had the tweezers and probe and one of those small weirdly shaped speculums (he unconsciously clenched his buttocks when he saw this duo).

"Ah. Here we go," he said as he grabbed a small scalpel.

Feeling a little more confident with his paper pants and a mini scalpel, he began walking slowly around the room, sliding his hands over the smooth wall. He was looking for any imperfection, anything that might indicate a door. A crack would do. On the last wall, the one that he couldn't see clearly from the gurney, he found a faint seam right behind Jamie's gurney. Up close he could see the line, but from even a few feet away it was invisible.

"There you are," he whispered. "I knew there had to be a door."

Marc was not unfamiliar with the way locks worked. He had learned many skills while growing up in the ghettos of Argentina. Maybe now those skills would serve a purpose. Picking a spot on what he thought was the edge of the door, about where a latch would be, Marc pushed the scalpel into the seam. He pushed and wiggled the small knife, but it couldn't seem to work itself in far enough to catch any mechanism. The blade was thin enough, but the handle was too wide to fit in the tight space. Marc slammed his fist into the door causing the material of the door to vibrate with a high-pitched hum. There were no scratches on the door where he'd shoved in the blade.

"What the hell is this thing made of?" Marc said out

loud, stepping backwards and bumping Jamie's gurney.

"Oopsie," Jamie giggled.

Marc turned to look at her.

"Jamie?"

Jamie was grinning. "You go bump."

Marc was stunned. This was the first time Jamie seemed to acknowledge him. "Yes, Jamie. I did." He swallowed hard. "I did go bump." He took a step close. "Jamie, do you recognize me?"

Jamie didn't reply. She sat there smiling and staring off into the distance.

Marc sighed. He'd hoped she was coming back; he could use the help.

The door was a dud. There was no way he was getting through there. He scanned the walls, looking for a weakness. The wall was seamless but worn, with spots of pale grey cinder block showing through where paint had been chipped away.

"Damn it," thought Marc, "I'm in a fucking sealed box. I don't want to end up like George or, worse, like you, Jamie. Nothing personal."

Marc scrubbed his hands through his hair; his wife's face popped up before his eyes. "Aww babe, I need to get back home to you and time is running out."

Whoever had kidnapped them would be back and every minute wasted was a minute closer to their return.

"Maybe I can cut through the wall?" Moving to a dark corner and squatting close to the floor, he proceeded to run the scalpel down the wall. His plan was rough: score the wall with the scalpel, marking out a rough rectangular shape big enough for him to crawl through, then kick out the drywall and get himself and Jamie out. It would be noisy, but it was the only option he had.

Holding the scalpel tight, he slid it down the wall. The blade made a horrible screeching noise, like nails on a chalkboard, as he slid it down. "What the...?"

Leaning in closer he could see it was made of the same strange material as the door.

"Fuck. Fuck, fuck, fuck, fuck, fuck."

Angry and frustrated, Marc stabbed the scalpel into the cheap laminate countertop and ran his hands through his shaggy black hair. He'd hoped to make his escape quietly and quickly, but he felt that he was running out of time and energy.

"I guess the door is my best bet," he muttered, pulling the blade from the surface.

Marc returned to the door and kept working at the area where he thought the lock would be located. Suddenly, there was an audible click and Marc jumped back in surprise as the door slid open. Bright light blinded him, and he raised his arm to shield his eyes.

"Tut tut, Marc. It isn't nice to destroy other people's property."

Marc knew that voice. Lowering his arm and squinting into the light he could just make out a familiar face peering back at him. With an eerie smile the figure raised its hand and sprayed something into Marc's face. He staggered back, coughing; it smelled like lemon cleaner. A wave of dizziness washed over him, and he stumbled back against a gurney.

Tony entered the room with that same evil grin fixed on his face and nonchalantly approached Marc.

"What the fuck are you doing?" Marc said, scrubbing at his eyes.

Tony gave Marc a pitying look. "That, I'm afraid, would involve a lengthy explanation and I simply do not have the time."

"Why?"

"There is no escape," was Tony's only reply.

Marc raised his arm holding the scalpel and took a futile swipe at Tony. Tony stopped just outside Marc's reach and the swing went wide.

"Now, be a good boy and get back on your bed. Things will go much smoother if you'd just co-operate."

"Jamie? Help?" Marc pleaded, making Tony laugh.

"She'll be of no help to you."

Jamie slid off the gurney behind Tony. She looked confused. After a brief glance at Marc, Jamie's eyes locked on Tony's back and she began to walk stiff-legged towards him. Marc was surprised to see her respond but it gave him hope.

"Fuck you," Marc snarled. He tried to balance himself better against the gurney. Stars floated before his eyes and his legs felt like jelly, but he was determined to keep Tony's focus on him.

"Now, now," Tony scolded. "I do believe Jason is having a negative effect on you, but he won't for much longer."

Jamie was right behind Tony and Marc had to fight the urge to smile. "Where Jason?" Marc slurred. Whatever Tony had sprayed him with was making it hard to speak.

"Jason isn't your problem," Tony said. He was patient. He could wait for the sedative to drop Marc to the ground. Marc was athletic, a body builder. Even with his enhanced strength, Tony would be hard pressed in a fair fight against the larger man, and Tony hated him for it; but no one could withstand the aerosolized version of this sedative. Tony just had to stay out of reach.

Jamie was moving better now, and Marc could no longer stifle his grin. Tony looked surprised at this. "What are you smirking at?"

"You," Marc said simply. Jamie wasn't a big woman, but he'd lay even odds on her against Tony any day.

The grin slipped from his face as Jamie walked past Tony and quickly closed the distance between them. She wrapped her arms around him and pulled him upright. "Jamie?" he wheezed as she squeezed the air from his lungs.

"Put him back on the table, my dear," Tony said as Jamie lifted Marc's one hundred and eighty pounds as if he was a bag of potatoes and plopped him down on the gurney. He struggled weakly as she held him down while Tony put the straps back on so tightly that they cut into Marc's skin. Once he was secure, she stepped back robotically.

Marc managed to focus enough to look into Tony's eyes. There was nothing behind them. They were dead. Soulless. Fear gripped Marc, adrenaline surged, helping to negate the sedatives effects. He shook his head. "Whadda you want?"

"You, Marc, just you," he said as he patted Marc on the arm.

Tony stepped from Marc's field of vision. "Now be a good boy and stop struggling."

He returned holding a petri dish filled with the same jelly-like blobs Marc had seen by Jamie's gurney. As Tony held it over Marc's face, he could see that the blobs were semi-translucent worms swimming in the clear fluid. Each worm was about half the size of a dime. Tony placed the dish on the tray and removed the cover. He picked up one of the speculum-shaped tools and turned towards Marc.

"Now, Marc, stay still. This won't hurt at all," Tony said with a smile that promised exactly the opposite. Marc tried to turn his head away but with a flick of Tony's hand, Jamie stepped forward and held his head in a vice-like grip. Tony slipped the speculum up one of Marc's nostrils, making Marc gag and his eyes water. Marc heard a click as Tony pulled the trigger expanding the blades. Marc yelped, and Tony laughed.

Marc blinked the tears from his eyes as he tried to see what Tony was doing. Tony turned around from the tray and was gently holding one of the worm-like creatures in the tweezers and carefully laid the cold, wet creature on the warm sensitive flesh just above Marc's lip.

Tony caressed the thing with a finger. Marc felt it wriggle at the touch and he shuddered.

Tony leaned in close and for one brief, irrational moment, Marc feared that Tony was going to kiss him, and he pulled his lips tight. Instead, Marc felt Tony's breath brush his mouth as he said, "Go, little one."

Marc felt the worm wriggle its way up his face and into his nostril. His eyes went wide with horror and tears streamed down his face. "Jamie, please, help?" he whimpered.

"The Jamie you knew is gone," Tony said. "You could

say she received an upgrade."

Marc looked at Tony, his eyes wide in terror.

"You'll understand soon enough. Or not." Tony patted Marc's arm once again and peered down at the terrified man with hungry eyes. "We'll see which it is in a few minutes."

Marc could feel the creature sliding its way through his sinus cavity. He wanted to throw up. After a few minutes he lost where it was. He hoped it had died. It hadn't. It had worked its way further up his sinus. It kept going until it reached the sphenoid sinus cavity, just in front of the midbrain.

That is when the pain began, and Marc started to scream.

CHAPTER TWENTY

Amanda was wide-eyed and breathing hard when she returned to find Jason huddled in a corner vigorously rubbing his arms to stay warm.

"Did you find anything?"

"Yeah, a few things," Amanda said as she looked nervously up and down the corridor.

"Everything okay?" he said, taking the clothing from her as she handed the pieces to him.

"Yes," she said before shaking her head. "No."

"Which is it?"

"I ran into Tony."

"Shit."

"Yeah. He knows what I'm doing."

Jason's face blanched. "What makes you say that?"

Amanda recounted her inopportune meeting with Tony.

"Do you think he suspects enough to change your access key?"

Amanda paused and frowned. "I don't think so. His last words were that I had to bring you here tonight or that Walter would take my place."

"You don't sound certain."

"I'm not," she said.

"We'll find out soon enough."

Amanda nodded and took another glance up and down the corridor. "Hurry. We'll have to change here where it's darker. It's too risky in the open."

"In front of each other?" Jason sounded horrified.

She turned to look up at him. "Jason, it's not like we haven't seen each other naked before."

"Yeah, but that was before…"

Amanda flushed red. "Before you knew what I am," she finished for him.

They were suddenly both very awkward.

"How about we turn our backs to each other?" Jason suggested.

Amanda nodded, her eyes downcast.

They turned their backs to each other as they began to strip off their wet clothes.

They could hear each other shuffling and a pile of damp clothes grew by their feet. Jason paused when Amanda's pink lacy bra fell against his ankle, still warm from her body. He swallowed hard and looked at the wall in front of him as he dressed. The alcove was small and occasionally they would brush an arm or shoulder against the other. Muffled apologies quickly followed as they'd try to retreat closer to their corner. Finally, they were both dressed and turned back towards each other.

"I don't think we'll win any fashion shows," Amanda said, eyeing Jason.

His wet auburn hair looked almost black, and the grey zombie t-shirt was a fit perfectly showing off his muscles.

Blushing, she quickly moved her eyes from his chest. The red plaid fleece shirt hung loosely. It was meant for a much larger man. The jeans were both too short and hung from his hips, bulging under his belt. One blue sneaker and one white one finished his ensemble. She grinned. "You look like a hipster lumberjack."

Jason snorted a laugh and despite himself said, "I think you look pretty good." Amanda beamed. Her clothes reminded Jason of the first time she'd stayed over and borrowed some of his clothes to sleep in. Her blond hair had begun to curl into ringlets as it dried, and the t-shirt was too small and emphasized that she wasn't wearing a bra. The track pants were too long so she had pulled the cuffs up, exposing her calves. Jason swallowed hard.

"Liar," she said, a small shy smile on her face as she turned away from him and picked up the pile of wet clothes.

Jason watched her as she shoved their wet clothes into a corner. She was risking everything to help. He knew that and part of him wanted to hug her for it, but another part wanted to scream at her here for all the things she'd done. Instead, he did neither.

She stood holding both their cell phones. Water drained from the corners. "I don't think these are going to help us much."

"No. Just toss 'em with the wet stuff." Jason sighed and continued, "Where do we go?"

"This way," she said, pointing further down the service hallway as she stepped from the alcove. "Walter said that Tony was going to the labs and he was headed that way when he left me."

They talked in hushed tones as they crept down the corridor. "Labs?" Jason asked.

"Yeah," Amanda replied. "There are research and experimentation labs."

"What would you be researching?"

"Research on adapting a planet to Acanthans. Improving the Acanthan integration process. Things like that."

"Adapting a planet? You mean terraforming?"

"Yes. Except I guess it would be Acanthaforming? We like it warm and wet."

"All that rain…"

Amanda nodded as she led them down the hall. "Yeah."

"Humans don't."

"We've realized that. Only some parts of the planet will be altered to accommodate the true Acanthan form. Mostly around the equator."

"Oh." He paused "Do I want to know what you mean by integration process improvement?"

"Probably not," shed said, shaking her head. "The, um, examining rooms are just past the labs," she said as they reached a door holding a swipe card and fingerprint reader.

"Pretty heavy security for a call centre backroom," Jason observed. "I'm surprised no one has ever noticed."

"They did."

"Do I want to…"

"No," she said flatly. "This leads to a short hallway with the two labs on the left and two examining rooms on the right. There is also a door to the printing and distribution floor further down the hallway." Amanda dug her pass card out of the track pants pocket.

"The examining rooms are where we implant our off-spring into the new hosts. Some people handle it okay enough and leave only hours after the process. They may be a little confused or disoriented. Others take longer. Those are left in the rooms to recover. Marc will be in one of the examining rooms." Turning to look up into Jason's eyes she said, "Jason, if he's been processed, he may not want to come with us, or he might try to turn on us."

Smiling sadly at Amanda, he shrugged. "I know, but what else can I do?"

Turning away from the pained expression on Jason's face, Amanda swiped her card and held the thumb of her left hand to the scanner.

With a soft click the door unlocked. Amanda grasped the handle and turned it easily, opening the door to reveal a brightly lit corridor.

"Remember, labs are on the left, processing is on the right," she whispered over her shoulder.

"What about security?" Jason whispered back.

"None. We never even considered that a human could figure out what was happening here."

Reaching behind her, she pressed her hand to his chest. She felt the warmth of his body and his heart beating against her palm. Taking a deep breath to steady herself she said, "Let me go in first. If Tony is there, he'd be expecting me. I'll leave the door open and try to distract him. Then you can... well... do whatever it is you are planning on doing." She paled a little.

Jason's face was hard as he nodded to her.

CHAPTER TWENTY-ONE

Amanda stepped up to the first door on the right and swiped her card to open it, glancing quickly around. The poorly lit hospital ward style room was completely vacant. Amanda sighed and shut the door as quietly as possible. She moved on to the next door. "Voices," she mouthed back at Jason and tipped her head to listen.

Motioning Jason back against the wall, she stepped up to the door, closed her eyes to centre herself, squared her shoulders, lifted her chin, and put an expression on her face of arrogance. Jason was speechless at the transformation. She swiped her card and the door opened with a click. She pushed it open and walked inside.

Tony stood with Jamie by his side.

He had his hand on her shoulder as he smiled down at the thrashing form of Marc, who was crying out in agony. Amanda recognized Jamie's blank stare. She'd had difficulty with the transition and was lost, but she'd make a perfect drone. Open to suggestion and good for mundane tasks.

Glancing around the room she saw George's limp body. He was undoubtedly dead.

Tony didn't immediately notice Amanda's entry into the room.

"There you are, I've been looking everywhere for you," Amanda said. She glanced down at Marc and continued, "I thought he'd have been done by now."

Tony slowly pulled his eyes away from Marc, who was writing in agony before him. Glowering at Amanda over the tops of his glasses he said, "There were delays. Why were you looking for me?"

"I can't seem to find any ketamine. I told you I was going to bring you Jason. I need the drug for that."

"It should be in Lab 2."

"It's not. I was just there."

"Damn it. I do not want any further delays."

"Well, as soon as I can sedate him, I'll bring him. Unless you propose I knock him over the head with something and hope for the best."

"Harumph," Tony grumbled, turning to look at Marc, whose cries had reduced to whimpers and his writhing to twitching with an occasional spasm.

"Everyone else is still here. We're trying to get the last few shipments out. I *need* Jason to finish the damned program. That idiot that Walter found can't program his way out of an Xbox, let alone write a program that can be sent via telecommunications devices." He took a break from watching Marc's suffering and looked up at Amanda, who had walked further into the room. "I had wanted it to be a surprise for you." Tony seemed excited. "We are so close to completion. We're just days away. All we need is Jason to be one of us so he can finish off the program."

Amanda was shocked. "Days? I thought we were

years from readiness?"

Tony waved his hand dismissively.

"Oh, the signal may not get to every human. That was somewhat inevitable as there are swaths of the planet without any cellular or radio service, but we will get many. Once they are under our control, they will be easy to process." Tony licked his lips in excitement. "However, that also means some will need to be harvested the old-fashioned way, by going in on foot." He looked at Amanda. "It's been too long since we had a good hunt."

"I've never been on one."

"That's right, you were born here. It's very exhilarating. I think you will enjoy it."

"It sounds... interesting. You will have to teach me." She smiled at Tony.

"Our estimate is that once the program is complete, we can go-live within twenty-four hours."

"You *have* been industrious," Amanda purred. She walked up to Marc's bed and ran her hand over his arm. She could feel his muscles twitching beneath her fingers and his head rolled back and forth. His face was screwed up in pain and he made small whimpering noises.

Tony smiled proudly. "It will give us immediate control over approximately 85% of the population, including their leaders."

Amanda had worked her way to the head of Marc's bed. Tony suddenly stepped close to her and took her into his arms. She looked up at his sudden movement and gasped. Tony's eyes were ablaze with a fanatical light. "Amanda, then I am going to rule this world."

"Really?"

"Yes, and I want you to rule alongside me." His hands were clammy against her arms and his breath reeked.

Repulsed, Amanda broke free from Tony's grasp, swatting his hands away. She managed to look down on him while looking up at him.

"No," she said coldly. "I would never be your concubine. You disgust me."

Tony's jaw went slack with shock, which quickly turned to rage. He was quivering with it. Amanda saw a vein throbbing in his temple as she pressed home.

"You say The Council will make you king? Will they still feel that way when they see how much difficulty you've had containing one simple human?" Contempt dripped from her voice.

She turned to look down at Marc, her face softening, and gently stroked his face. Marc's thrashing quieted to mild twitches and shudders as Amanda touched him.

She'd managed to turn Tony to fully face her, his back to the door. He was impotent with rage and for a moment she feared she'd pushed him too far, that he'd kill her before Jason could act.

Her dismissal of his offer and the way she was touching Marc was too much for the egomaniac to cope with.

"Your love of these creatures is disgusting. They are nothing more than beasts."

"You seem to enjoy some of the perks of humanity," Amanda sneered.

Tony's eyes bulged and his whole body quivered with fury. No one had ever had the audacity to speak to him like that.

"You bitch. You'd choose the likes of him over me?"

Tony waved at Marc's prone form.

"Oh, I haven't chosen Marc at all." Amanda smiled at Tony, her eyes flicking to just above his left shoulder.

Tony didn't miss that look and spun around just as Jamie squealed, "Jason," and clapped her hands. Tony stopped Jason's fist with his face. Almost twice the size of the scrawny Tony, Jason sent the man flying into a tray, sending utensils flying in all directions. A petri dish shattered on the floor. Dozens of small worm creatures wriggled in the shallow liquid as it ran down the floor drain into the sewer below. Tony fell to the floor, blood running from a broken nose, his lip already swelling where it was split.

"Help me get him up on the empty gurney," Amanda said, grabbing Tony's legs while Jason went around to grab his arms. Tony was Acanthan and wasn't so easily subdued. He grabbed a handful of tools that had fallen from the spilled tray, and as they bent over him, his eyes opened, and he drove a set of forceps deep into Jason's arm.

Jason recoiled, grabbing at his wounded arm, and stumbled backwards. With a cry he gripped the forceps and pulled them free.

"You traitorous bitch," Tony snarled at Amanda through his swelling lips which gave his words a slurring lisp. He held a scalpel that he'd found on the floor before him. Amanda scrambled backwards, her hands held up in front of her to fend off any attack.

"Jamie," Tony said and the woman's blank face turned towards Tony. "Restrain Jason."

"Jason." She said and took a step towards him.

"Jamie, no. Stop." Amanda ordered.

Jamie hesitated.

"Jamie, I'm your Master. Obey me." She moved towards Jason again.

"Jamie, this is you commander." She summoned all her authority and ignored the fact that she was scrabbling across the ground. "It's Amanda. You will cease action and stand ready by the wall."

Jamie spun on her foot and walked to the wall where she stopped, turned and sat, with her back to the wall."

"Fuck it. I'll deal with Jason myself. Right now, I will enjoy killing you."

"Tony…" Amanda started, glancing over at Jason, who was holding the hole in his arm, blood seeping from between his fingers.

"Shut up," Tony snapped, waving the blade at Amanda. He'd managed to get to his knees and was crouching like a trapped animal, ready to spring.

"That trick won't work again." He stood and went over to Marc, placing the blade at his throat. "First you will watch your friend die."

Jason had also managed to stand and was holding the forceps in his good hand.

Amanda spoke quickly. "Tony, you're right. I am a traitorous bitch. I've betrayed the entire Acanthan population here on Earth. I deserve to die."

She pointed to Marc's recumbent form. '"He's just survived processing. Marc's smart and strong. Don't waste a valuable resource just to get even with me." She swallowed hard before continuing, "Take me instead. I'll go peacefully. Just let Jason go."

"Amanda, no," Jason said, horrified.

Tony hesitated. He glanced at Jason, who was staring at Amanda slack-jawed.

"Please, Amanda, you can't."

"Jason, I can. I will." She looked Tony in the eye. "Well?"

Tony looked at Amanda and a horrible smile parted his ruined lips, his bloodied teeth making him look like a vampire.

"Very well," he said as he lowered the blade from Marc's neck and beckoned Amanda to come to him.

Jason looked from Tony to Amanda. He was a long way from forgiving her, but he could clearly imagine Tony sliding the scalpel across her throat and he was not about to let that happen.

As Amanda took her first steps towards Tony, Jason threw the forceps at Tony's head with all his strength. Tony's head turned reflexively as the forceps' tip hit, biting deep into his face, tearing a long gouge. His hand flew to his head as blood began to run.

"Fuck!" Tony screamed. Blood sprayed over Marc's face and gown.

"Fuck." Jamie parroted and then let out a chilling laugh, making Tony hesitate as he looked at her.

Jason saw his moment and dove, taking Tony at the hips in a football tackle, driving him to the floor. The force of the blow drove all the wind from Tony's lungs. As they skidded to a stop against the cabinets, Jason had rolled away, but Amanda stepped in with a heavy utensil tray in her hands. Raising it above her head, she brought it down on Tony with enough force to leave a Tony-shaped dent in the metal.

"I choose Jason."

Tony slumped to the floor as Amanda dropped the tray and ran to Jason.

His arm was bleeding badly.

"Are you okay?" she asked.

Jason was secretly pleased at the worry in her voice.

"I'll live." Jason nodded towards Tony. "Is he dead?"

Amanda glanced back at him and said, "No, but he's out cold."

"Good. What about Marc?" Jason said as he batted Amanda's hands away and tried to wrap the edge of his plaid shirt around the injury.

Amanda looked over her shoulder at Marc. He was mostly still now, but he looked pale in the washed-out lighting.

"He was processed."

"I got that. Is he going to live?"

"I think so."

"Can it be reversed?" Jason looked from his friend to Amanda. It killed her to tell him the truth.

"No. Any separation will kill the human host."

"What about the Acanthan?"

"Yes and no. If another host is ready, we can be transplanted but we won't survive long without a host." Amanda looked at the blood soaking through Jason's improvised bandage.

"We've got to get you patched up. We can deal with Marc after. He's not going anywhere."

As much as he hated to agree, Amanda was right. He was bleeding a lot. He was a little concerned that Tony had nicked an artery. "Are there any bandages in this place?"

Amanda nodded and jumped up, heading to the cabinets on the wall. When she returned Jason was sitting on the empty gurney with his plaid shirt pulled off and was carefully examining the hole in his arm. It wasn't large but it was deep. Any other time he'd have gone for stitches, but they would have to wait.

Amanda laid out her supplies: a bottle of antiseptic, gauze squares, and some tape. She took Jason's arm in her hand. He resisted.

"Please, Jason, you can't possibly do this one-handed. Let me help."

He hesitated before relaxing, allowing her to pull his arm out straight. She examined his wound.

"You need stitches."

"I know."

"I can do them."

"No. There's no time. Patch me up."

With a sigh she took the bottle of antiseptic in her hand.

"This is going to hurt."

As she spoke, she poured the liquid into the hole. Jason hissed through clenched teeth as the peroxide fizzed and burned. Once it stopped, Amanda wiped the wound clean, closed it as best she could with some Steri-Strips, wrapped it in fresh gauze, and taped it up. The whole process was done in minutes.

As she finished, her hands slid down until she was holding his hand in both of hers. "Amanda–" Jason began.

She dropped his hand and shook her head. "Not now.

We've got to deal with Tony."

It was Jason's turn to feel hurt, but she was right. Tony wouldn't stay unconscious forever. Between them, they hoisted Tony onto the gurney and tied him down with the restraints that he normally used to hold his victims. They used torn strips of one of the hospital gowns to make a gag and then covered his whole body in a blanket.

Once he was secured, they tidied the room as much as possible, taking a few moments to cover George with a sheet, and moved him and Tony over to the side. They hoped if anyone looked in, they'd think it was two corpses ready for disposal.

Jamie had watched the end of the fight without much as flinching. She'd remained sitting while the trio fought.

Jason finally had a moment for Marc. He walked over the prone figure of his friend, who was now murmuring and muttering in his sleep, eyes moving rapidly behind closed lids.

"They really got to him, didn't they?" he asked without looking at Amanda. He'd hoped she had been wrong.

"Yes," she replied, stepping up next to him.

Patting his friend on the shoulder he said, "I'll be back for you."

Amanda looked up at Jason in surprise. "What do you mean back? I thought we came here for Marc."

"We did. But I heard what Tony said to you about being nearly ready." Jason turned to look at Amanda. "I can't just run."

Amanda couldn't answer that; she knew what the plans were and what would happen.

"I'm not the only programmer. They will find someone to replace me and finish the code. It may take longer but they will. Then what? I hide while my entire planet is taken over?"

Jason was getting angry again. She could feel it starting to radiate from him in waves.

"What kind of life is that? This is my planet. It's my people. I have to try."

"What can you do?" Amanda asked, her voice shaking.

"You mean what chance does a pathetic human have against the Acantha?"

"That's not what I–"

Jason cut her off with a wave of his hand. "It doesn't matter. I have a plan."

As Jason talked, Amanda could see a change coming over him. He was always quiet, somewhat shy, not outspoken, and certainly not aggressive. Now he was angry, and that rage fuelled his determination. He wouldn't go down without a fight.

Jason smiled grimly. "Well, I've got some skills. I'm going to use all that shit I learned in school. First of all, I need to get into that douchebag's office," he said, nodding towards Tony's prone form.

"Then I need to raid a janitor's closet. I'm also going to need containers, preferably glass or something that will break easily." He had a far away look as he thought and planned; his eyes had a shine of anticipation. Amanda was a little disturbed by the enthusiastic glint in his eye as he spoke.

"Last, where is the electrical room?"

"Jason, that's a lot of sneaking around."

"Yes, it is."

"Is there anything I can say that will change your mind?"

"No."

"I didn't think so." Amanda had a sense of déjà vu wash over her as she recalled their conversation out on the pier. "Okay. Fine. I'll help then." She smiled at him. It was a lopsided, resigned smile and, for the first time, Jason smiled back.

"Thank you," he said quietly.

"Okay then, Tony's real office is in the hallway, closest to the call centre floor. With almost everyone out in printing or distribution, it shouldn't be too hard to get there unseen."

Amanda nibbled her bottom lip as she thought, and Jason caught himself smiling down at her. He quickly reminded himself that this thing wasn't Amanda.

"There's also a janitorial closet on the way, so that makes things a little easier. I'm pretty sure there's a bunch of mason jars in the lunch room..." She paused, thinking. "The electrical room is slightly more problematic. It's on the other side of the printing centre, which is now filled with my fellow Acantha. What are you planning?" Amanda asked.

Jason looked up at Amanda. "I'm going to out-human these fuckers."

CHAPTER TWENTY-TWO

They made their way unobstructed to the janitor's closet. Switching on the light, Jason smiled at the cornucopia of chemicals before him. Immediately he grabbed a bottle of ammonia, bleach, drain cleaner, and, after a quick reading of the label, three large bottles of floor wax.

"Slide the mop and bucket over," Jason said. "We're gonna need some glass jars too. And a roll of tinfoil if there is one, or anything with aluminum."

She raised her eyebrows in question but did as he asked, pushing the large yellow bucket over to him. Jason poured two full bottles of the floor polish into the tub of the scrubbing bucket and piled the bottles of cleaner onto the ringer.

"We're taking it with us," Jason said, and Amanda wheeled the bucket and mop combo into the hallway. As Jason was shutting the door, he spied a beat-up old ball cap hanging on a peg. On a whim he grabbed it and stuffed it into his back pocket. Pushing the bucket before them, they made their way to Tony's office.

The lights were off, and the door was ajar. Their luck was holding; there was no one around. Slipping inside, Jason sat at Tony's computer. He felt a momentary pang of regret: it was a beautiful laptop, easily worth at least four grand, and it broke Jason's heart a little when he though about what he was planning to do to it.

Jason brought up the login screen. "Damn it. It's password protected. Do you know it?" he asked Amanda.

"No. He never trusted anyone," she replied as she looked around the desk for anything that Tony may have written the password on.

"Okay, you have some of his memories, right?"

"Yeah. A few older ones…" Amanda replied pensively.

"What are some things he may have used as a password?"

Amanda frowned as she thought.

"He's a creature of habit, narcissistic, and a megalomaniac. One of his past ones was Epic1."

Jason keyed in the password. "Nope. Try again."

"Dominator123," Amanda suggested.

"Strike number two," Jason replied. "We've only got one shot left before the system locks us out."

"He must be using a new one," Amanda frowned. "Try IndependenceDay1."

Jason raised his eyebrow.

"He said it's his favourite movie."

"You sure?"

"No, but it's the best guess I can make."

He started to key in the password when Amanda grabbed his arm. "No, wait. Try SlaveMaster70Vir."

Jason looked at her with raised brows. "That's random."

"Not if you know Tony." Amanda frowned. "He's bragged about Acanthan superiority and that he's going to be humanity's slave master. 70Vir is the Earth name given to the star that Acantha orbits. Tony would think this is funny."

Jason shook his head; Tony was way more fucked up than he'd thought. With a flick of his fingers, he entered in the password and they both held their breath. They sighed audibly when the screen flickered for a moment before it finally cleared to show a black background with a glowing red electronic eye peering out and the caption "HAL: It can only be attributable to human error" in white font below it.

"Seriously?" Jason said to Amanda, pointing to the computer screen. "HAL9000?"

Amanda looked at him blankly.

"It's from *2001: A Space Odyssey*. Can an invading alien actually be geekier than a human?"

Amanda shrugged. She only had the vaguest idea of what he was talking about.

"Great job," Jason said as he started clicking on files and doing a quick perusal before moving on to the next.

"Not really," she said.

He stopped his searching and looked up at her. Grinning sheepishly, she held up a post it note with the password printed on it.

"You had it the whole time?"

"No. I just found it. It was stuck inside his planner."

Shaking his head, he went back to work. While he worked on locating the files he wanted, Amanda slipped out to the cafeteria to find his requested containers, shutting the door behind her. She found dozens of them kept in the fridge and cupboards, which she emptied and quickly wiped out before stuffing them into a backpack she'd pilfered from the lost and found.

Nearly a half an hour passed before Amanda slipped back in to Tony's office.

"Jackpot," Jason said.

Amanda was surprised to see him pulling a USB drive from the laptop.

"Where'd you get that?" she asked.

"I'm a computer geek," he replied with a grin, as he started to close down all the files he'd opened.

Amanda looked at him in disbelief.

"How... where... We were soaked."

"Okay, I found it in the pants pocket."

"The ones got from the lost and found?" Amanda looked at Jason, surprised.

"Yep, the same. And outside of some porn, which I deleted, it was blank."

She shook her head.

"Almost ready," Jason said.

Grinning like a Cheshire cat Jason put the cover back on the USB stick and stuffed it into his pocket. "I copied as many of Tony's files regarding the invasion to the drive as I could. It has a lot of information on Acanthans, how you got here, images of your species, info on how processing works. There are also files on every person that was processed. From Tony's CloneZone account, I emailed the information and what amounts to a recorded confession from Tony to every major newspaper worldwide, the FBI, CIA, Homeland Security, and ICE."

"Tony had recorded a confession?"

"No. It looked like he recorded every meeting. I picked a couple and got lucky on the third try. It was one between him and Walter where he did a full evil villain monologue. It was perfect."

"I wasn't there?" Amanda looked into Jason's eyes questioningly, holding his gaze.

Jason turned away. "Not on the one I sent."

"Is Jason trying to protect me?" Amanda thought to herself. "If so, why? He's made his dislike of the real me clear."

She wanted to ask him, but he continued before she had a chance.

"I also got into Tony's social media accounts and posted it there." Jason paused and looked at Amanda. "He had freaking social media accounts. Who'd have guessed?"

"We all had some, we had to keep up appearances."

"It worked."

Amanda didn't know how to respond to that, so she simply laid the bags of jars on the desk.

"Perfect," Jason said.

"What if no one believes it?"

"What?"

"The stuff you sent out."

"Well, that would suck, but it won't matter in the end. I've got a coup de grace."

"What are you?"

He was grinning from ear to ear. "Tony said I was good and he's about to find out just how good I am." Jason paused and looked up at Amanda. "With the info sent out, we probably don't have a lot of time left before the shit hits the fan."

Amanda suddenly put her finger to her lips, silencing Jason. She stuck her head out the hallway and looked up and down. There was nobody there. "I thought I heard something. We need to hurry before someone shows up."

"Just gimmie another minute. I'm going to need a couple more things."

Jason began digging through Tony's desk, grabbing a pair of scissors and stuffing them into his pocket. Once he'd grabbed what he thought he might need he took the polish-soaked mop from the bucket and spread the polish liberally around Tony's desk. Amanda paled. "What are you doing?"

"You'll see."

"Jason-"

"No time to explain, we have to hurry. Remember?"

Amanda nodded.

"What do you need?"

"Those labs we passed..."

"What about them?"

"You said they did genetic research."

"Yes."

"There's gotta be test tubes, sample vials, or something similar. Right?

"Yes. Why?"

"I need them."

Amanda thought briefly about trying to dissuade Jason, but when she saw his look of grim determination, she knew there was no point.

"C'mon," Amanda said, leading the way into the corridor. Jason followed, slopping polish from the bucket as he went. He shut the door behind them and headed the short distance to the labs, dragging the sopping mop behind him. The first lab they came to had a sign on the door that read "Genetics." She swiped her card and the door unlocked. Amanda turned the knob and opened the door, letting bright light spill into the hallway. Jason and Amanda squinted against the harsh light.

"Commander?" a baritone voice greeted her. "I wasn't expecting you."

"Jerome? Why are you still here?"

"Oh, you know the Captain." There was a chuckle. "He wants the latest numbers on the next gen, and if I don't get them to him, and I quote, 'by yesterday,' there will be hell to pay. He's put a major rush on the research."

"Yes, I certainly do."

Amanda nodded her agreement as she stepped into the room, motioning Jason to remain in the hallway. The room was lit with bright halogens and she wrinkled her nose at the smell of sanitizer and formaldehyde. It always made her think of mothballs. The walls were flanked with scientific equipment: a centrifuge, a DNA sequencer, microscopes and more; there were two metal desks facing each other at opposite ends of the room. Jerome was seated at the desk that was against the far wall.

"Have you seen the Captain?" Jerome asked. "I was expecting him earlier."

"I believe he's a little tied up with one of the processings." Amanda put on a disappointed expression. "It didn't go as planned, I'm afraid."

"Oh, that is unfortunate. Was it a valuable asset?"

Amanda nodded. "Yes. The Captain is displeased."

Jerome nodded back with an expression of mutual understanding.

"Who's that with you?" Jerome said, pointing vaguely in Jason's direction.

"A drone."

Jerome raised an eyebrow.

"Actually, the Captain sent us," Amanda interjected before Jerome could ask any further questions.

"Really?"

"Yes. He sent us to retrieve some specimen vials."

Jerome stood and went to a nearby cupboard. He took out a tray of small glass vials, sealed with plastic stoppers. "Will this do?"

"Perfect," Amanda said, smiling as she reached for the tray.

Jerome pulled them back and held them close as he looked back and forth between Amanda and Jason suspiciously. "It is my job to collect any specimens. What does he need them for and why did he send a Commander for such a menial job? And with a drone to help?"

"They are for specimens. I do not answer to you, therefore the why is none of your business."

"Specimens of...?"

She was beginning to sweat. Why was Jerome suddenly so suspicious? He was usually a rule follower, not one to question a superior's requests.

Amanda sighed melodramatically and replied brusquely, "If you insist. It's for a dead Acanthan's brain tissue. From the failed processing I told you about."

Jerome frowned. "The Captain would have normally just used the intercom to request me to come and take the samples. I am the one who normally does any necropsies. The Captain dislikes getting his hands dirty."

"There is an issue with the intercom."

"Then why send you and not a drone?" Jerome had stepped back to his desk and was reaching for the intercom button, regardless of the fact that she'd said it was not working.

She glanced out in the hallway and could see Jason crouching slightly, ready to do what had to be done. She made her second gamble for the night. She stepped closer to the desk and frowned.

"Jerome, I'd hoped to spare you this until we knew for sure. You are a damned good geneticist and an asset worth retaining."

Jerome's hand stopped a centimetre away from the button. "What?"

"Tony was going to page you, but..." Amanda shook her head. "You wouldn't have enjoyed it if he had." Amanda looked sad and disappointed. "I told him it wasn't your fault. That the host had been faulty, not the symbiote."

Jerome blanched. "What do you mean?"

"The specimen he needs to sample is from the failed processing tonight and he blames you."

"Me? How?" Jerome's hand fell away from the intercom and he paled.

"Well, it is *your* next gen that killed the host."

"Oh." Jerome looked a little green as he sat down heavily in his chair.

"Tony wanted to punish you right away, but I convinced him to let me do the necropsy. You are our best geneticist."

"I told him they weren't ready. That the recoding was not stable. There was a high risk of death instead of generating a drone that is nothing but a husk with augmented physical capabilities."

"Oh, sweet Jesus," Amanda thought, fighting back a rising dread. Tony had used a next gen on her friends. As she thought of Marc her eyes flicked briefly to Jason before turning her focus back to Jerome. He was so distraught she could have likely started tap dancing right in front of him and he'd not have noticed.

She pressed on. "Have you ever known Tony to be patient?"

Jerome shook his head.

"The Gen2 samples were ready and he had a host. That's all he needed to know."

"Why did he choose such a high value host?" He was visibly sweating now.

"He likely felt the benefits of having this asset as a Gen2 were worth it. We did have assurances that they were viable, if a little unstable." Amanda shrugged. "Other than that, why does Tony do a lot of the things he does? If you want, you can ask him that the next time you see him."

Jerome looked up at her in shock and shook his head vigorously. "No. I don't think I will."

"While I am a more patient person than Tony, my patience does have a limit and I'm beginning to regret my decision to help you." She extended her hand for the tray. "Now, if you want, you can go ahead and page him or you can give me the vials and we can pretend you weren't here when I showed up."

As Jerome held the tray out, the vials rattled a little as

his hands trembled.

As Amanda left, she said over her shoulder, "If I were you, I'd lock myself in here and get that report ready." She paused briefly. "And it had better have very good news."

She closed the door behind her and nearly collapsed when she heard it snick shut.

"Fuck." She gaped as Jason grabbed the vials and held her by the elbow, steadying her.

"You were amazing," he said, looking down at her. She looked up into his sparkling green eyes and smiled weakly.

"I want to puke."

Jason smiled in sympathy. "Welcome to humanity."

CHAPTER TWENTY-THREE

Amanda parked the bucket and mop by the door as they re-entered the room. She sighed as she saw that Jamie was standing exactly where they had left her, still playing with her gown. What were they going to do with her? She next checked on Marc. He was still out cold, but he was no longer twitching or crying out. His breathing was slow, steady, and peaceful.

"He's sleeping," Amanda said as she joined Jason where he sat on the floor, laying his spoil before him.

Jason set the bottle of bleach and ammonia next to each other then paired up the drain cleaner and the roll of tinfoil. As he worked, he glanced at Amanda checking on their friends and he thought, "She played that geneticist. She controlled whole thing right from the minute she opened the door. How many times has she done that to me?" He thought back to all the times she'd asked something of him, and he'd complied, almost without protest. Their first date, moving in together and getting him to work at CloneZone. He shook his head to clear it. He had to focus on what he was doing. A mistake now could be fatal.

He sat cross-legged on the floor and grinned like a kid with his first chemistry set. He started by lining up all twenty-one mason jars and split them between the bleach and drain cleaner sides.

"Chlorine first," he said under his breath.

"What are you making?"

"Grenades."

"What?" Amanda sounded horrified.

"I hope I don't have to use these, but I need something in case I'm caught." He looked up at Amanda and said, "I won't be turned."

Jason carefully began to half fill the first ten of the jars laid out before him. Once that was done, he took the smaller specimen vials and filled them with ammonia, capping each one carefully with their rubber stopper.

He carefully wiped them clean and lowered each one into a bleach-filled jar and sealed it. With that task completed he turned to the other set of jars.

He handed the roll of tinfoil to Amanda. "Can you tear this into tiny pieces and fill the specimen tubes with it?"

"Ummm, sure."

"Don't pack it tight."

While Amanda did as he'd asked, Jason filled the remaining jars with drain cleaner.

Once again, he carefully lowered the vials into the murky liquid.

Before sealing these, he looked at Amanda and asked, "Anything not made of aluminum that we can put in?"

"What for?" Amanda looked confused.

"Shrapnel."

"Oh," she said, her voice subdued.

"The ones with the drain cleaner will be, more or less, frag grenades. Once the cleaner mixes with the aluminum, it will explode. Anything inside becomes shrapnel. They aren't powerful enough to kill, but I want them to make an impression."

Jason looked at her as she stared at the bottles arrayed out before him. "Second thoughts?"

Amanda's eyes rose from the jars to Jason, slipped around the room taking in Marc, Jamie, and George, and finally rested on the form of Tony for a moment before she looked back to Jason. She tried to smile; it was small and wavered.

"No." Her voice cracked. She cleared her throat and said firmly, "No."

"Good." Jason returned her smile.

Amanda stood and found a box labelled "sharps," which turned out to be about two hundred lancets. Small and wickedly sharp. Jason shared them liberally amongst his drain cleaner jars. Using latex gloves as barriers, he screwed the caps onto the jars.

"What are the other ones?" Amanda asked, pointing to the bleach-filled bottles Jason was stowing back into a backpack.

"Ammonia chloride," he replied.

Amanda just looked at him blankly.

"They are chlorine gas grenades. It's nasty stuff. When the ammonia and chlorine bleach mix, it releases chlorine gas. It will burn the eyes, nose, and throat."

"But it won't kill, will it?"

"Oh yeah, it can kill." He looked down at the bulging backpack. "Once this is done, I hope there isn't any evidence that this is what I used."

"What do you mean?"

"It's banned by the Geneva Protocol. I'd go to jail for life."

"Jason." Amanda was horrified. "You can't."

"I can." He held one of the gas grenades before him, slowly turning it around. The pale-yellow bleach swirled a little and the tiny vial of ammonia made a muffled clink against the glass. "I have to."

He put the jar in and stood, hefting the pack onto his back.

Jason looked down at his watch. "I need to hurry. We've been in here too long. They are soon going to start wondering where Tony is."

Amanda nodded then opened the door and checked the hallway. It was clear. She stepped out and tugged the bucket away from the wall and stood there holding the mop handle in her left hand. In her right hand she held her ring key along with her key card.

Jason stepped up close to her and held out his hand for her keys. "This is it, I guess. Do or die time?"

"Don't say that." She looked up at Jason longingly. "Please."

"It's just a figure of speech. Trust me, I have no plans on actually dying."

Jason's heart lurched as he looked into her eyes, as if seeing her for the first time. He didn't know if he was suffering from some bizarre form of Stockholm Syndrome, or maybe he was finally seeing the real Amanda.

Hesitantly, he touched her cheek.

She pressed her face against his hand. Reluctantly he took his hand back, and reached into his pocket, withdrawing the USB drive. Taking her hand in his, he laid it in her palm and closed her fingers around it.

Holding her hand Jason said, "Take this. I want you to get Marc and Jamie, then get out of the building."

"Jason, no."

"Please. I can't do this unless I know you and Marc are safe."

Amanda's heart was breaking; he couldn't do this to her. Give her hope that there could be something more, then throw his life away. If he were caught, she had no doubts about how this would end. It was selfish, but if he died, she'd have no one, nothing.

"Let me help you," she pleaded, her eyes filling with tears. "You stand a better chance with me."

He smiled down at her sadly. "No. A couple of hours ago you told me you loved me."

"I do," Amanda said. Jason could feel her hands trembling inside his own.

"Then save my friend. Get him back to his wife and kid."

"Jason…"

"Please, Amanda."

Tears threatened to slip from her eyes and her voice failed, but she nodded.

Jason turned to leave, but at the last moment he paused. He didn't want to leave things like this. Just in case. Impulsively, he leaned in and kissed her. He stood and pulled on the ratty ball cap he'd found in the closet and began to "mop" the floor. He headed straight for the printing floor, smearing liberal amounts of floor polish around as he went.

CHAPTER TWENTY-FOUR

Amanda re-entered the lab to find Tony awake, wiggling and mumbling through his gag, and Marc semiconscious. She pulled down the sheet from Tony's head revealing the large purplish bruise that had developed where Jason had punched him. Tony's eyes went wide when he saw her looking at him. She stood there, staring down at him, seeing the pure hatred in his eyes.

"I'm sorry," she whispered, "but I can't leave you here."

Relief flooded Tony's face as Amanda reached for the gag.

"Thank you," Tony croaked, his mouth was dry from the cotton gag.

Tony glowered at her. It might have had more effect if his face hadn't been so swollen. As it was, it only made him look demented.

"I knew you'd come to your senses." He still had a lisp from his swollen lips. "No one needs to know what happened here. Of course, you will be punished, but not severely, and your lapse will stay between us." Tony's voice, while still a little horse had grown increasingly commanding as he spoke. "Now, untie me and help me up."

Amanda looked from Tony and back to Marc, whose eyelids were fluttering. "He's coming around," Amanda thought. She glanced at Jamie and wondered if there'd be any of the old Marc left. She could still feel Jason's kiss and the warmth of his breath on her neck as he said good-bye to her.

She looked back down at Tony and said icily, "I think you misunderstand me."

Tony's eyes went wide with incredulity. "What did you say to me?"

"I said 'I believe you misunderstand.' I do not want to help you and I will not leave you here," Amanda replied, squaring her shoulders. She looked Tony defiantly in the eye. "I've tolerated you for years. Your groping hands and your creepy leering looks. I've done all you've asked but it stops here. I hate you. You're a narcissistic power-hungry bastard."

As she spoke Amanda reached behind her to the instrument table and grabbed something that felt like an ice pick.

"Today I am human," Amanda growled as she swung her arm around, plunging it into Tony's neck. Warm blood spurted out over her hand and she quickly yanked it away. Tony tried to scream, but it came out as nothing more than a gurgle. He started to choke as blood poured down his throat and filled his lungs. His wide eyes looked accusingly at Amanda as she pulled the sheet back over his head. He twitched and thrashed as blood soaked the white sheet.

Jamie yelled out, "Cantaloupe," and giggled.

Amanda looked at Jamie sadly and sighed. She looked down at her trembling, blood-covered hands and wanted to throw up. Grabbing a corner of the sheet, Amanda scrubbed the blood off. She wanted to curl into a ball and cry. She felt weak. These feelings weren't what she'd expected. Guilt, sadness, remorse. She hated Tony. She thought it would have been easy, but Amanda had never taken an Acanthan life before, and it was taking a far greater toll than she'd ever anticipated.

Marc moaned, drawing Amanda away from her thoughts.

"Marc, can you hear me?" she asked, turning her back on the blood-soaked sheet.

"Wha... what happened?" he asked, trying to sit up.

As much as she knew Jason cared about Marc, Amanda had no intentions of releasing him until she determined whose side he was on.

"Marc, you, Jamie, and George were taken by Tony. He may have done things to you. Do you remember?" she said.

"Amanda? Is that you?" Marc said, squinting to try and bring the amorphous blob that was his friend into focus. "It's not safe. You have to get out of here."

Marc tried to lift his hand to rub his face and found that he was still restrained. Suddenly everything came rushing back to him: Jamie, George, and Tony.

Marc's eyes were wide with panic.

"Oh my god, Amanda, it's Tony. He gassed us. He killed George and fucked Jamie up. Please help me?"

"Shhh. Marc. It's all right. Calm down. Jason sent me

to help you, but I need you to tell me, what do you re-member."

"Jason? He's alive? Where is he?" Marc looked around frantically for his friend.

"Yes, Jason's alive." She didn't add the little thought of "for now" that had popped unbidden into her head. "He's doing something. You need to answer me."

"Amanda, please unstrap me before he comes back," Marc begged as he jerked against the restraints. He was just barely holding his panic at bay. Flashes of Tony's gloating face, the feel of the thing on his face, and the pain flitted through his mind.

"Marc, I promise I'll help you, but you need to an-swer me. It's very important." Amanda steadied herself. She was scared and precious time was passing. "Listen to me, I don't have time to explain everything right now, but Tony used an anesthetic gas. Did it smell like lemons?"

Marc nodded.

"That's Sevoflurane. It works fast, but once you wake you are fine."

"I don't feel fine."

"I don't suppose you do. He was experimenting on people. Before I can untie you, I need to make sure that you're... you." Amanda held onto Marc's face, forcing him to look into her eyes. "Tell me everything you can remember."

Marc looked into Amanda's eyes, searching for any-thing that indicated she was involved. He hadn't forgot-ten the box that held her signature. Amanda saw his fear and suspicion. She couldn't blame him after everything he'd been through.

"Marc, you can trust me."

"Really? Where's Jason?"

"He's gone for help."

"Jason would never leave you."

"Marc, please–"

"No, Amanda. Now. Something isn't right here. Let me up."

"I have to confirm something first. Please. It's important. Tell me what happened, and I promise I'll undo the restraints."

Marc knew he was trapped. Amanda had the upper hand. What was she trying to find out? He was afraid to answer. If she was part of this, he was screwed. If she was really trying to help him...

"Fuck it," he finally muttered, defeated. He turned his head to look at her.

"The truth?"

She nodded.

He shuddered recalling the feeling of the creature on his face.

Taking a deep breath, Marc said, "I know it's going to sound crazy, but Tony put a weird slug on my face, and it crawled up my nose."

"And then?" Amanda prompted.

"You believed that?"

"Let's say I do. What happened next?"

"Then it felt like someone had poured acid into my brain. I think I passed out. Next thing I know I hear voices and you are standing next to me." Marc looked at Amanda. "Who were you talking to?"

"Jamie," she replied absently, puzzled by Marc's lucidness. If he'd been processed, he should be having problems remembering and talking.

"Marc, are you taking any drugs?"

Marc looked at Amanda as if she'd lost her mind. "No."

"Prescriptions, anything at all? It doesn't matter what or how insignificant."

"Well, my doc has me on a nasal spray for sinusitis. It wasn't really working though."

"Fluconazole?"

"Yeah, I think that's it. It's in my jacket pocket, wherever that is."

"Marc, fluconazole is an antifungal. It may not have cured your infection, but it saved your life," Amanda said. Grabbing Marc by the cheeks she kissed him right on the mouth.

Marc's eyes popped open wide.

"Whaph?" he mumbled around her kiss.

"It's is also used to treat N. fowleri." Smiling with relief, Amanda began to undo the restraints holding Marc in place.

"N flowers?"

"No, N. fowleri. A brain-eating amoeba."

"A what? Tony tried to kill me with an amoeba?"

"Not really, but something similar to it. I'm sorry I didn't untie you right away. I had to be sure it was really you and you hadn't been changed."

"Oh, I'm changed all right. I'll never be the same again," he said as he sat up.

Jamie clapped her hands and squealed, "Watermelon."

Marc attempted to stand, putting his arm around Amanda for support.

As he made it to his feet Amanda said, "I don't feel right leaving Jamie behind."

"I'm okay with leaving her. She helped Tony recapture me. We can't trust her."

Amanda sighed but she knew Marc was right. If Jamie was following Tony's orders it was only a matter of time before she became a liability. She opened the door and stepped out into the hallway. Behind them they heard the distinctive sound of a gun being cocked. The pair turned slowly. The barrel of a '45 was only inches away from them and it was shaking.

"I think Tony may want a word with you two."

CHAPTER TWENTY-FIVE

Quietly, Jason closed the heavy door behind him. It shut with a quiet snick that felt very final to Jason. Thoughts of Amanda and Marc almost made him turn back. They were his friends, and he was abandoning them. He paused with his hand on the knob and looked back over his shoulder at the grey metal. Maybe he should escape with them and let the authorities deal with Tony. He'd sent them everything they'd need, and he'd given Amanda the USB with everything he'd had time to transfer. It was enough. Why did he have to do anything else?

Jason thought of George's corpse, Jamie's loss of sanity, and Marc's whimpers of pain after whatever Tony had done to him. So much was at stake. If the authorities didn't believe the email or saw it too late, then Tony would succeed.

Taking a deep breath, he turned his back on the door and stepped forward. He couldn't turn back now.

He paused to look around. He'd never been in this part of the building before. Nothing was familiar to him and while Amanda had given him the layout, he really wasn't sure where anything was. Time was precious, but he couldn't just go blundering around.

The room was expansive, a wide open warehouse. He couldn't see much thanks to the stacks of paper and printing materials that turned the open space into a maze. The place reeked of oil, toner, and ink.

Off to his right, he could see the huge loading doors; they were closed. They were also his goal. Next to them was a door he planned on using for his escape.

He'd have to circle the perimeter without being seen. His plan was to box the creatures in, to get as many as he could.

That thought turned his stomach to ice. He'd never killed anything in his life and now…

He sighed and took a quick furtive look around. Jason allowed his shoulders to slump, pulled the hat he'd found down further to mask his red hair, and kept his face down while he slowly worked his way between the printers and packaging machines, slopping floor polish in his wake, hoping no one would notice he wasn't the usual night maintenance man.

Adrenaline pumped through his veins, his heart raced, but Jason felt more alive than he'd ever felt in his life. Even if he was only mopping a floor. He'd always played it safe, never taking a chance, never really lived. He vowed that if he survived this, things were going to change.

Carefully he worked his way through the floor leaving a slug trail of the polish. Polish was the perfect incendiary. Even if it dried, the fumes were flammable. The over-stuffed backpack filled with hastily prepared drain cleaner and bleach grenades he'd made dug painfully against his back. He sent a silent prayer to whatever deity would listen that the grenades stayed stable until he needed them. Otherwise, he'd take himself out in a most unpleasant way.

"At least these bastards will come with me," he thought morbidly.

Jason worked his way through the warren of stacks, leaving puddles of polish as he went. At intervals he'd hold the sopping mop up against the flammable materials, soaking them in the hopes they'd go up like Roman candles. He grinned when he came across a pallet filled with canisters of printing toner with their small warning labels with a flame. Here he poured some of the polish, saturating the floor and wooden pallet.

"That'll get their attention." He moved slowly, avoiding Acanthans, as he worked his way around. It felt like an eternity but in reality it didn't take him long to reach the electrical room. It was right where Amanda had said, located against the far-left wall of the huge room.

Bringing the mop and bucket with him, Jason used Amanda's key to open the electrical room door and slipped inside and shut it behind him. It was pitch black. He fumbled around the wall until he found the switch and flicked on the light. The single bare bulb flickered to life.

The room was fourteen feet long and twelve wide and had been used as a maintenance and storage area. Piles of boxes, wiring, and supplies lined the walls, casting shadows. It was like something from a horror film. The room where the serial killer always caught the pretty girl.

"Friggin' creepy," he said with a shudder as he stripped to the waist and tore his cotton t-shirt into ribbons, throwing the pieces into the bucket of polish to soak. Pulling the black button-down shirt back on he turned his attention to the series of panel boards on the far wall. He quickly read through the menus that ran down next each of the circuit breakers, a variety of lights, outlets, and security doors. With each passing tab, he began to worry that the one he was looking for wasn't there. He moved to the final panel in the row. It was a much smaller panel that connected to the others by a grey conduit pipe. It had a faded label that read "Loading Doors."

"Never fails. It's always in the last place you look," Jason said with a wash of relief.

He'd been afraid they wouldn't be together, and he'd have had to search the whole floor. He'd never have been able to do what he needed to in time if this switch had been out in the open.

Jason grinned and pulled the lever down until it clicked, cutting power to the panel. His goal was to cook alien brain-eating slugs, not to electrocute himself. The panel was locked, but that was okay; he didn't need to access the panel directly. All he needed to do was get into the set of wires leading from the panel to the door.

Another, smaller plastic conduit tube ran from the bottom of the subpanel. About a foot below the panel there was a join where it turned and ran parallel to the bigger conduit tube above. This was the weak point he needed. Jason gave it a tug, but it didn't budge; it was fixed solidly to the panel and the cinder block wall.

"I've got to find something to break it or pry it off," he said to himself as he looked around the room. He quickly found a toolbox poked behind a few stacked boxed of maintenance supplies. Pulling it into the light he discovered it was locked with a small padlock.

"Seriously?" he muttered. Hoping no one would hear, he picked up the toolbox and slammed it against the wall until the small lock fell to the floor, still attached to the double loop. He put the battered box down and foraged inside it.

"This should do the trick," he said as he stepped back to the panel with a claw hammer in hand.

He needed to break the pipe but not mash the wires inside. He raised his arm and gave the plastic a whack. It cracked and splintered but not enough. He jammed the hammer in behind the pipe and gave a hard tug. It loosened and more plastic tinkled to the ground.

The final blow shattered the plastic, exposing the black-coated wiring inside.

There was a knock on the door.

"Shit." Jason jumped at the sound. His heart raced as he looked around frantically for a place to hide while the doorknob wiggled back and forth.

"Hey, who's in there?"

The boxes would never conceal him.

He heard the soft snick as the door unlocked.

Jason jumped behind the door as it opened and hid it its shelter, holding the hammer tightly in his hand.

"Hello?"

The figure stepped in front of the door. It looked down at the bucket filled with rags.

"Who the fuck left this here?" He began to close the door. Jason knew once the door closed, he would been seen.

"Me," Jason said, stepping forward, hoping to bluff

his way out. Just in case he couldn't, he kept his right arm tucked behind his leg, hiding the hammer from view.

"Jason?"

It was Gary, the pimply drug dealing dude. Even as an Acanthan he smelled faintly of cheap weed. The look of surprise was quickly replaced with a look of smugness Jason recognized; it was the same look Walter and Tony would get just before they turned your life to shit.

"What are you doing in here?" Gary said, looking at Jason suspiciously.

Jason started down at the shorter man, his mouth suddenly dry, while his heart beat frantically and beads of sweat stippled his brow like tiny pearls.

"I didn't know you had joined us?" Gary asked.

"Ah, yeah. Last night."

"Humph. They don't tell us shit."

"Not much different than working in the call centre," Jason said, laughing nervously.

Gary nodded. "Ain't that the truth. Looks like you had it easy if you're on your feet already."

"Yeah, everything went smoothly. Bit of a headache and a nosebleed but that's it."

"You're damn lucky. I was out for days. Felt like I was dying." Gary shrugged indifferently. "But I didn't end up a veg or a slab of meat, so it all worked out."

Jason blanched. "Yeah. Lucky."

"Guess we should get going," Jason said as he moved to step around Gary, thinking he'd have to double back for his supplies. He felt a hand on his arm.

"What are you doing in the electrical room?"

"Umm," Jason stuttered. "Amanda asked me to check

on something. I'm an engineer. So, she thought I could help."

"Right," Gary said, the doubt clear in his voice.

"I'm serious. See?" Jason held up Amanda's badge and keys. "She loaned me her stuff since Walter hasn't bothered to get mine ready yet."

Gary looked back and forth from the badge to Jason's face. He was close enough that Jason could smell the marijuana on his breath.

"Yeah, that makes sense. Walter is so busy crawling up Tony's ass it's a surprise he gets anything done," he said with a shrug, his hand dropping from Jason's arm. "If I see Tony, I'll let him know I was talkin' to yah."

"Sure thing," Jason said as the two stepped outside the room, Jason starting to close the door behind them.

"Don't forget the big meeting tonight," Gary said over his shoulder as he walked away.

"Meeting?"

"Lemme guess? They didn't tell you."

Jason laughed quietly. "Of course not."

"Tony has some big announcement. Wants us all to meet at ten."

"Great. Yeah, thanks. I'll be there," Jason said as he watched Gary's back fade into the shadows.

Jason took a deep breath and turned back into the electrical room, shutting the door behind him.

He looked at his watch, it was almost nine. "I'll have to work quickly now," he thought as he returned to the toolbox and took out a heavy screwdriver, which he used to pry the thick wire a little way out of the conduit. With still trembling hands he tried to carefully peel back the outer coating to expose the bundle of wires inside.

Jason teased out a single red wire and, using the scissors he had taken from Tony's office, pared back the cover to get the copper beneath. With a little effort he tugged the wire further out of the tube, allowing it to dangle close to the bucket. He used the screwdriver to get the sodden strips of cloth from the bucket and piled them on the wringer. He then positioned the bucket right under the panel.

"Shit," he muttered, the wire wasn't low enough.

He looked in the toolbox and saw a wrench. He pulled it out and wrapped the copper around the wrench, letting it dangle just above the soggy mess. He stepped back to appraise his handiwork and nodded his approval.

"MacGyver would be proud."

When the switch by the doors was turned on to open the bay doors, it would complete the circuit and cause the wire to arc, sending 20,000 volts into whatever happened to be handy. Right now, what was handy was the pile of rags soaked in highly flammable floor polish over a bucket filled with the same polish.

"Boom," he whispered as he grinned and made the universal sign for explosion.

Jason then turned the breaker back on, carefully picked up the backpack, took the mop, and dragged it behind as he went, leaving a trail of polish that looked like a giant slug had passed by. He turned off the lights and left the door slightly ajar.

A good fire needs air.

CHAPTER TWENTY-SIX

Walter forced Amanda and Marc into Tony's office and tied each of them to chairs. He called Tony's cell and tried to reach him using the intercom, but there was no response. With each failed attempt, Walter grew more and more agitated.

"C'mon, Tony, where are you?" he muttered as he turned back towards his prisoners.

When he saw the smug look on Amanda's face he snarled, "What have you done?"

She refused to answer. Instead, she shot Walter a look of pure condescension. Without warning he slapped her, rocking her head to the side. A trickle of blood ran from her lip. With a smirk of defiance, she spit the bloody mess into his face. Walter went florid with rage. He raised the gun to her face. She could see down the barrel as it sat millimetres from her nose.

"You will tell me what I want to know."

"Leave her alone," Marc roared, struggling at his restraints. Walter turned to look at him and grinned before turning his attention back to Amanda.

"I know you will not succumb to torture, *Commander*,

but your friend here has had no such training."

"Commander?" Marc's struggles ceased as he looked from Walter to Amanda and back again.

"Marc, I'm sorry. It's complicated." Looking past the barrel of the gun, she stared directly into Walter's eyes before continuing, "We can't tell Walter anything."

"Aw fuck." Marc's shoulders slumped. He knew what was coming and mentally braced himself for the blow which rocked him back in the chair. Blood ran from a gash over his eye. More blows followed. One after another rained down on him, each one eliciting a cry or pained grunt. He felt a rib crack, the wind was knocked from his lungs, his lips began to swell. His attachment to consciousness became a thin thread.

After what felt like an eternity, he heard Amanda screaming and the hits stopped. His head lolled back and forth and bloody spittle dripped from his open mouth. He heard Amanda saying words, but they held no meaning for him.

From a distance he heard a door open and close. He thought he heard crying, but he wasn't sure what was real or if it wasn't his own tears. His eyes closed as he allowed himself to slip into the abyss and all sound ceased.

Jason worked his way around the building, working hard to avoid anyone, occasionally passing by pairs or groups close enough hear them talking. He never lingered to listen. He'd just tuck his head down and mop, betting on the fact that no one ever paid attention to a cleaner.

Their voices followed him. Haunted him. He looked down at his hands where they clutched the mop handle.

He saw a little grime around his nails where he'd rigged the wires, but otherwise they were clean. After tonight he wouldn't be able to say that.

He stopped walking to pool some polish around a case of toner. He didn't know how combustible the toner would be, but it would burn dirty making a cloud of toxic smoke.

A laugh echoed through the air. Jason hesitated. A lump formed in his chest. He knew the consequences of what he was doing. Did he really have to? He turned to look at the slug's trail of polish in his wake. He could go back. It would only take him a minute to change the wiring back. Then leave. Never look back. Make sure the cops got the USB drive, knew about what was going on here, but he'd have no part of whatever happened to everyone.

He recalled what was on that drive, what he'd seen on Tony's computer. He'd only had time to transfer the highlights, hopefully enough to interest the authorities, but he'd seen more. Pictures of the unsuccessful, images of the creatures stuck to a human brain. Once you'd been processed, there was no going back. You weren't human anymore. You were a hybrid.

A monster.

With a heavy sigh Jason began to mop again. He had no choice. The police were a hope but no guarantee. He was here.

Now. He had to act.

Jason moved on, slopping the polish wherever he went. He soaked piles of paper and pooled the polish around more jars of toner, working his way around the building. Meter by meter he drew closer to his goal, the loading bay doors.

"I'm gonna make it," he thought. For the first time since he developed the plan, he felt real hope that he'd make it out alive.

A roar of cheering stopped him in his tracks. He stood there, frozen, listening as a familiar nasally voice rose above the din, punctuated by a scream of pain.

"It can't be."

CHAPTER TWENTY-SEVEN

Amanda struggled futilely against her bonds. Whatever could be said about Walter, he made sure his prisoners were secure. A quick glance at the clock on the wall confirmed her worst fear, their time was running out.

"Marc." He was unresponsive and his head hung against his chest.

"Marc?" she called, a little louder. He'd been through a lot and had taken one hell of a beating. Walter hadn't pulled any punches, and when he'd started pistol- whipping Marc, she'd caved.

Walter knew where Tony was, and he was gone to get him. It didn't really matter, Tony was dead.

Amanda looked at Marc closely. His chest rose and fell with even, steady breaths.

They still had a chance. She just had to get free. They didn't have much time before Walter would get back and when he did both their lives would be forfeit.

She worked her wrists against the zip tie bonds, feeling them cutting into the tender skin around her hands.

Her hopes faded as she heard the door open. Amanda turned to look, her stomach sinking as she saw Walter helping Tony into the room. Tony was deathly pale and had a heavy bandage wrapped around his neck, making him look like he was wearing a turtleneck.

"It's good–to see–you–again, Amanda," Tony wheezed, a tight smile spreading across his thin lips.

"How?" Amanda felt ill.

"I am not–so easy–to–kill." His words came in short panting gasps.

"I found him and gave him this," Walter said proudly, holding up a heavy syringe. His obsequiousness was sickening.

"I saved him."

"Yes–you–did." Tony patted Walter on the shoulder. He looked like a proud pet owner praising his faithful dog. She wouldn't have been surprised if he'd taken out a biscuit and fed it to Walter.

"What is that?"

"Oh, a little–something–from–R&D."

Tony gasped as he collapsed into his chair.

"It boosts our ability to heal," Walter finished for his boss.

Tony looked from Amanda to Marc, who appeared to be regaining consciousness.

"Now…" he wheezed. "Now you get–to be Earth's–first example of what happens–to traitors."

His speech was getting stronger by the moment. Amanda paled. "What are you going to do?"

Tony just smiled and said, "Walter, escort our guests–to the gathering."

Walter smiled. "My pleasure."

CHAPTER TWENTY-EIGHT

Jason couldn't make out a word the voice was say-ing. He caught snippets that sounded like "traitor" and "betrayal." He had to get closer. Carefully, he worked his way around from behind the bench, walking along the fringe of the crowd slowly. They were shuffling and mov-ing about in their growing excitement.

As Jason drew nearer, he had to fight the fear that was threatening to overwhelm him. The blob on the end was certainly Walter, the other was Tony; he had to know if what he suspected was true. Using the stacks of boxes as cover, he finally found a position where he could clearly see the improvised stage.

The world lurched beneath Jason's feet as his worst fears were confirmed. He could see both Marc and Aman-da on the bench with Tony. Marc was the shadow stand-ing next to Walter who was holding a gun to Marc's head. Marc's face was a mass of bruises. One eye was swollen nearly shut; his expression was blank.

"What have they done to you?" Jason thought as he looked at his helpless friend.

Anger replaced fear when he saw Tony holding

Amanda by the hair, her body pressed against his and a scalpel hovering perilously over her carotid artery. A trickle of blood ran down Amanda's pale throat where the sharp blade had bit into her soft skin. Her hands were bound tightly before her with a black zip tie. Jason could see where the plastic had cut her.

As he moved, he heard more and more of Tony's words, that whiny, nasally voice sending a shudder down Jason's spine.

"She killed the innocent. The helpless. Jamie and George were like newborns. They could do nothing to help themselves," Tony cried as he moved Amanda forward.

All eyes turned to her as the crowd hissed and roared.

"Listen to me," Amanda called out, beseeching to her fellow Acanthan's. "He's lying."

Tony glowered and prepared to strike when a voice called out, "Why would the Captain lie?"

"He wants power. All of it," Amanda responded. "You don't matter to him. We're disposable. Look what he's doing to me?"

"Yes, look at what I'm doing," Tony cried. "I'm bringing a human-loving traitor to justice."

"You were caught trying to help him escape," Walter said, using the gun to point to Marc. "But it was too late, so in a fit of rage you attacked us. Killed Jamie and George."

"I did no such thing," Amanda screamed.

Leaning, Tony whispered in her ear, "They'll never believe you. They're mine."

He then lifted his head and called to his followers, "She lies."

"Liar. Liar. Liar." The mindless mob echoed their master.

Her eyes flicked from face to face, hoping to see a glimmer of doubt. But there was nothing. What little hope she'd had fled.

Jason gritted his teeth when he saw Tony lean in close and whisper in Amanda's ear. She looked like she may vomit but remained still. It wouldn't take much for the scalpel to end her life.

Putting on an expression of false concern, Tony nodded towards Marc. "This poor soul has just been processed. He may be misguided or confused." He shook his head sadly. "So, I will withhold judgment on him. For now."

Jason's heart sank, his worst fear realized. He'd held out hope, but he'd been too late.

Tony gave Amanda a hard jerk, making her yelp as he pulled her hair, the scalpel cutting another fine line.

"This bitch I know for a fact is a traitor to our cause."

Angry fists waved in the air. Cries of "Kill her!" echoed across the floor.

"Oh, we will, my friends. But first you need to know all her crimes." Tony paused for effect. "She has been conspiring against us."

An angry rumble began to rise. More voices joining the chorus of hate. Punctuating Tony's words every time he gave pause.

"She, Marc, and Jason have been working against us for some time and tonight they attempted a coup."

Tony's face remained grim as he waited for the din to die down.

"As bad as those crimes were, our Amanda, your Commander, my Second, my own daughter forsook me," Tony lowered the scalpel from Amanda's throat as he ripped the bandage from his own to display an ugly puckered scar on either side of his neck.

"She tried to kill me," he screamed.

Jason looked from Amanda's face to Tony's. He had to be lying. He'd been unconscious but alive when Jason had last seen him. Bound and gagged, but very much alive. Amanda wouldn't have done that, would she? Jason didn't want to believe it, but there was Tony looking like a mockery of Frankenstein's monster with its bolts pulled off.

Amanda turned her head slightly to look at Tony then spoke loud and clear, "My only regret is that I failed."

The crowd was enraged. Jason was sure if Amanda fell from the bench, they'd have torn her apart.

Tony smiled; she was helping him.

"Fear not, my friends. The ever-devoted Walter has saved us."

Walter puffed up twice his normal size and grinned. Jason had never wanted to punch someone so badly in his entire life.

"Thanks to his dedication and diligence, the conspiracy is ended, and I have named him my Second."

The crowd cheered and applauded.

"Walter. Walter. Walter."

Amanda tried to pull free, but Tony pulled her back and put the scalpel to her throat once again. He waited, allowing Walter to soak in the glory. When he judged the time right, he raised his hand, quieting them.

"Now, friends. We have a difficult decision to make." He put an expression of sorrow on his face. "What are we to do with our Amanda?"

The simple chant of "Kill her" began again.

"Yes, of course," Tony said. "But I ask you friends, how?"

An unintelligible cacophony of answers ensued.

Tony smiled out over his followers. He could see the anticipation, the hunger, in their eyes.

"It must be a message to any who might consider following in her path." Tony paused briefly as he looked out over the sea of faces before him. Each one looking at him expectantly. Only he could guide them.

"Friends, human history is rife with ways to kill each other. They've furnished us with so many options to choose, it's hard to decide. We could hang her or burn her at the stake."

Tony smiled down at the fevered faces that looked up at him. "We could draw and quarter her or I think..."

He held out his decision for a moment, the crowd grew quiet in anticipation. Leaned in. Waiting.

"We will flay her."

The crowd erupted in one voice, "Flay her. Flay her. Flay her."

Tony beamed down at them. A proud father.

"She will remain alive until our conquest is complete. She will watch. She will know her failure to protect this pitiful species and despair."

Tony shuddered with anticipation as he finished,

"This will be glorious."

A cheer arose. The sound was filled with a primal need that made Jason's stomach turn, and he slipped the backpack from his shoulder. He looked around at the gathering. He saw Sue from accounts receivable who rescued kittens, Jerry who sat behind him and was the biggest comic book fan. Nearest to the stage he saw Gary the druggie. Faces he'd known, who'd been his friends. Now they were twisted with hunger and rage. A desire for blood. For the first time Jason truly saw them as the alien beings they had become.

His eyes blazed with anger as he pulled his ball cap down tight and stepped from behind the boxes. The crowd's inhuman screeching drowned out Jason's howl of defiance as he reached into the bag and pulled out the first grenade.

Amanda saw Jason. His face grim. Despite the proximity of the blade, Amanda tried to shake her head, but Tony's grip fixed her head almost in place.

Marc's head bobbed loosely but a smile slowly spread across his face.

Jason hung the bag on his left arm, keeping the top open, and withdrew the first gas grenade. He gave it a quick shake, breaking the small glass vial, allowing the drain cleaner and aluminum to mix. The glass became hot against his hand. He threw it with all the strength he could muster. It landed a few feet from the makeshift stage and exploded. Fragments of glass and burning chemical pelted those nearby.

They fell screaming. The second grenade Jason tossed flew towards the right of the gathering, shattering against a table and landing amidst the crowd. This one was a gas grenade. The bleach and ammonia mixed, releasing the green noxious chlorine gas that burned the eyes and throats of all those within its cloud. They too fell screaming, tearing at their faces as the corrosive chemicals blistered the eyes of those it hit. Clouds of the gas began to spread, choking and blinding the Acanthans wherever it went, while another drain cleaner bomb exploded nearby.

Tony looked on in horror as his people succumbed to the chemical attack. The floor below was nearly covered in the low hanging gas that moved and swirled beneath the stage. Like a hunting predator, its tendrils reached out, brushing its victims, weakening them, before enveloping and claiming them.

A man stumbled to the edge of the bench, his hands reaching up to Tony, his eyes beseeching.

"Help me?" Gary pleaded. His blistered and bleeding hands clawed at Tony's legs as he stumbled back, repulsed. Angrily he looked up to see where the grenades were coming from.

"Where is he?" Tony growled. As he searched the sea of faces, he yelled again, "Where is he?"

Amanda's bound hands grabbed at Tony's. "I don't know."

A scream of rage and frustration tore from Tony's throat.

CHAPTER TWENTY-NINE

Walter couldn't take his eyes from the cloud of gas that stalked him. The putrid yellow fog crept forward as he took several clumsy steps back from the rising fumes, distracted, his gun arm lowered. Without hesitation Marc spun, shoving the older man. Walter stumbled backwards, off the bench and onto all fours. The cloud of gas wrapped him in its embrace.

Screaming and writhing in pain, Walter tore at his face as the gas burned his eyes and seared his throat. Marc waited for a moment longer, watching as Walter began to twitch and cough up blood as the chlorine ate away his lungs.

"Pendejo," Marc snarled as he turned away from the dying man.

Jason saw the sudden movement from the bench and froze as he watched, slack-jawed with a bleach grenade held forgotten in his hand, while his friend took Walter down. "Marc?"

Jason couldn't believe what he was seeing; Marc had looked almost catatonic standing next to Walter. His blank face had been reminiscent of Jamie's vacant stare.

Jason's eyes flicked to Tony. A quick glance confirmed that Tony had seen everything.

"Marc!" Jason yelled, waving his arms and pointing to Amanda.

Marc scanned the crowd. A stationary bright red ball cap stood out amongst the panicking people and he followed Jason's frantic waves.

Jason cried, "Run!" and threw another grenade, managing to land it right in front of the platform holding Tony and Amanda.

Tony stepped back from the fumes, his eyes wide in horror.

"No," he gasped, backing away.

He looked wildly from the approaching Marc to Amanda before giving her a shove towards the edge.

She cried as she realized his intent and tried to dodge. She made double fists and swung at Tony, but she lost her footing. As she fell, her shoulder hit his hand and the scalpel scored a deep gouge along her back. Amanda screamed as she fell from the bench onto to the concrete floor, hitting it with a sickening thunk. Tony leaped over Walter's still form & disappeared behind the cloud of gas.

Jason started to run towards Amanda, heedless of the gas that separated them.

"Jason, stop!" Marc yelled as he ran, stumbling for Amanda, smoky green tendrils of gas on his heels. "I've got her."

A cloud of gas passed between them and Jason had to turn back or be burned.

CHAPTER THIRTY

Tony was blind with rage. He stumbled through the maze of the warehouse with his shirt pulled up over his mouth and eyes squeezed tightly shut. As quickly as he could, he made his way through the burning gas.

"Jason," he screamed as he stepped from the cloud.

The only response was the screams of panic and pain from his acolytes and the crash of breaking glass as Jason continued to lob his grenades. The warehouse was filling with more and more toxic gas, burning chemicals, and shrapnel. Chaos ruled.

Tony tore strips from the bottom of his shirt and tied it across his mouth while stuffing more around the edges of his glasses. Protected as best as he could, he began his search for Jason.

"The bastard can't be far." Tony was quivering with the desire to strangle Jason with his bare hands. Once Tony got a hold of him, he would pay dearly for this attack.

How many had he killed or wounded? Tony could see bodies littering the floor. Some still whimpered and twitched feebly, others were crawling away.

"I'm gonna kill you Jason. You'll pray for death before I'm through with you." Tony paused as a fit of coughing wracked him. Blood speckled his lips.

Jason heard the threats. He peaked from behind some boxes and scanned the area, looking for the source. He sighed, letting his head fall back against the boxes; he just wanted this over with.

A low keening wail drew Jason's attention. A blistered figure crawled from a cloud of low-lying gas. He shuddered a little in revulsion at the sight. He'd called Tony a monster for his acts of violence and cruelty, but now here he was doing the exact same thing to the Acanthans.

Jason swallowed bile and turned away.

He could just make out the doors and he slipped from his hiding place to make a run for it, but a new noise drew his attention. Tony had staggered out. For the first time since Jason had met him, he felt Tony's appearance matched the personality. He didn't seem to notice the swelling or blisters that covered a face that was screwed up in a rictus of rage.

"Jason," Tony called. "Where are you?"

Jason's only response was to toss his last frag grenade towards Tony. As he did, he broke cover and ran towards the delivery doors. He had to reach that switch. Jason coughed and staggered as he ran through a tendril of the greenish gas, nearly bringing him to his knees, but his eyes were on his prize. The ramp that led to a pair of buttons labelled "Open" and "Close." Jason kept his focus on the green "Open" button. The grating of the ramp echoed hollowly under his feet.

"I'm going to make it," he thought as he reached out

his hand to hit the button.

His fingertips brushed the button as he was slammed to the floor, the impact knocking the air from his lungs. A hand clutched his ankle and he was dragged down the ramp, the rough grating tearing skin from his ribs, arms and legs. Jason kicked at the hand. He had to get up. He had to get to the switch. He was so close.

He kicked. His foot made contact with something and he heard a yelp of pain and the hand released. Jason climbed onto his hands and knees.

"I didn't say you could leave." A whistle had joined the nasally whine.

"Tony." Jason stood, his hand gripping the railing. He turned to look at his adversary.

There was a trickle of blood from Tony's nose where Jason's sneaker had made contact.

"You know this was all pointless." Tony waved his hand in a sweeping gesture.

"How so?" Slowly Jason shuffled his feet backwards, working his way up the ramp.

"You've not stopped us," he laughed. "You haven't even really slowed us down. A few days, maybe a few weeks, at most."

"Slower is better," Jason shuffled a few more steps.

"You think you are the first creature to oppose us?"

Jason paused. He'd never even thought about that. With a shrug he replied, "I don't know."

"You aren't. Eventually all their races fell to us. Earth will fall too."

"You have no idea about humans, do you?"

"I do."

Jason laughed mirthlessly. "No, you really don't. You'll never *process* us all in time and we don't give up. Ever." Jason stumbled a few more steps, drawing ever closer to the switch.

"Amanda and Marc are both dead," Tony said suddenly. Jason staggered, his face blanching.

"I don't believe you."

"Your little bombs were quite effective. Perhaps a little too effective for your liking. I watched them die."

Jason's eyes filled, but he kept inching his way back up the ramp, Tony slowly following him.

"I watched them die." He shrugged. "It wasn't the execution I'd imagined, but their screams were music to my ears." Jason felt sick and his lips were white with the effort to say nothing. He was so close.

"Once you've joined them, I'll finish what I started. Your pathetic little planet will be ours."

Jason felt weak. Drained. Exhausted. He looked out over the warehouse floor; gas still churned and twisted, pushed by the air conditioning system. He felt the ramp edge under his foot. The platform itself was under his heel. He was only a couple of feet away.

Bile rose in his throat. His friends were dead. He was cornered. A desperate plan formed in his mind. If they were truly gone, well, he'd make their deaths count.

He looked at Tony. "You're wrong."

Jason turned, pushing off and diving for the button.

Pain. Jason's world was pain. An intense burning pain that seemed to radiate from his lower back. He flopped face forward onto the floor, his feet drumming a dull tattoo on the metal ramp. Jason could hear laughing. Confused, he reached his right hand behind him, and it came away wet.

"Blood? I'm bleeding?"

A pair of black loafers topped by white socks appeared before his eyes.

"I told you that you wouldn't win. You're only a human after all."

The pants rose above the end of the socks as their wearer crouched down and gently cupped Jason's chin in his hand, tilting his head upwards. Up close Jason could make out how much damage had been done to Tony's face. He could have been a grotesque from a travelling carnival's sideshow. He was bruised and there was blood matting his thin hair. Bits of glass peppered his face amongst the blisters that covered it like pimples. One eye was purple and swollen. Yet he loomed over Jason, triumphant and gloating.

"I win," he whispered.

Blood dripped slowly from a scalpel that he held in his swollen fingers. Weakness overwhelmed Jason and as Tony let go, he allowed his face to fall to the concrete. His vision went hazy and stars swam before his eyes. He could feel his life bleeding out with each beat of his heart.

CHAPTER THIRTY-ONE

Tony knew he had gotten lucky stabbing Jason in the back. It looked like he'd nicked one of Jason's arteries and it wouldn't be long before Jason took his last breath. He shrugged as he stood, letting Jason's face drop to the ground. He'd wanted to savour killing him, but this would have to do.

With a sigh Tony turned away to hunt for the other two banes to his existence, Marc and Amanda. He had no idea if they were alive or dead, but he planned on ensuring the latter sooner rather than later. He had a score to settle with Amanda, and he desperately wanted to exact his revenge.

A rictus grin of excitement distorted Tony's already disfigured face as he stepped off the ramp. He would take his time with her.

Jason knew he didn't have long. Staying conscious was getting harder with each breath. He watched Tony's feet disappear from view. Spots began to float before his eyes.

"And this is how everything ends? Not with a bang, but a whimper." With a sigh he laid his head down. "Didn't someone famous say that?" he wondered.

"At least I tried."

As he lay in a spreading pool of his own blood, Jason thought he saw Marc and Amanda, each leaning heavily on the other. He smiled. They were dead, but it was a nice thought, that they'd get away. Free for whatever time was left.

His imagination showed them creeping between towers of boxes hiding from Tony and the Acanthans who were trying to rally their forces. His oxygen-deprived brain was giving him a final gift before its final shut down. He watched them as they slipped from cover to cover. Jason closed his eyes. He'd soon be joining his friends.

"There they are."

Jason's eye opened wide and he struggled to focus.

"What?"

Now that they were closer, he saw the blisters on Marc's hands and the blood staining Amanda's shirt. He watched the surviving Acanthans closing on them.

"They're alive," Jason gasped.

But not for long if they were caught. Tony would use Marc and Amanda as examples. He'd make it as long and slow as possible.

Darkness was forming at the edge of his vision when Jason saw Tony appear and started creeping between the boxes his friends were hiding behind. He was hunting. Jason could see that he'd intercept them long before they made it to the door.

They would never make it out.

Tony stopped. He was a predator waiting for his prey, a razor-sharp metal claw clutched tightly in his hand.

Jason shot Tony a hateful look. Summoning what little strength remained to him, he pulled himself around and using only his arms crawled the last few feet, dragging his legs up the metal ramp. He felt nothing as they slid along the cheese grater metal.

"That's good at least," he thought.

Tony had finally done him a favour.

He looked over his shoulder and saw Marc and Amanda nearing Tony's position.

"Damn it," he muttered. He had to go faster. He pulled himself the last few feet to the wall and collapsed as stars swam before his eyes.

A scream brought him back and his eyes flew open. He looked around, confused. He realized he must have fainted. He didn't have much time. Frantically he searched for his friends.

His vision was blurry, but he spotted them. Amanda was on the floor. She had a new blossom of blood on the side of her shirt, but she was awake and crawling on hands and knees towards the small exit that was next to the loading doors. Marc was wrestling with Tony. He was a big man, but he'd been through hell today and Tony was Acanthan. He was buying Amanda time to escape.

Jason had to help. He closed his eyes to gather what strength he had left, then pushed himself up to sit, fighting back a wave of dizziness. He tried to reach the button from where he was but couldn't. His fingers could just brush the close button.

"Not fucking helpful," he growled.

He looked back to his friends. Amanda had made it to the door and opened it. She was holding the frame like a lifeline. He thought she was calling to Marc, who was still struggling against Tony. Jason could see he was weaker.

It was now or never. With a final heave he grabbed the railing and pulled himself up. He cried out as pain flared anew in his back. A wave of dizziness threatened to take him under, and black spots danced before his eyes. Gritting his teeth against the pain and dizziness, Jason threw himself forward, hitting the green button as he fell.

He collapsed hard against the wall and turned his head to watch.

There was a whooshing noise that came from the electrical room. The Acanthans all stopped and looked over their shoulders, Tony included. It gave Marc the break he needed. With all the strength he could muster he gave Tony a shove, sending him flailing to the ground.

Marc stumbled for the door, grabbing Amanda on the way.

The polish ignited, sending flames screaming throughout the centre. Volatile printing supplies transformed into accelerants. As the flames swept throughout the building, all the chemicals ignited, adding fuel to the inferno.

Small explosions could be heard above the flames as canisters under pressure burst, feeding the growing inferno. A secondary whoosh and a ball of flame soared, sending out clouds of black, choking smoke.

"The toner," Jason said with a weak smile.

All those who were standing on the newly polished floors caught fire as clothing ignited. Jason couldn't help but grin as he watched Tony stumble backwards from Marc's push. He'd landed in a pool of the polish. He stood angrily, his wet clothes clinging to his body. Jason watched as the wall of flame reached Tony and he went up like a Roman candle, screaming as his flesh burned.

"Acanthan superiority my ass, you arrogant mother fucker."

Jason began to laugh as he slid to the floor, his vision fading. The loading door had opened a few feet before the flames melted the wiring. It was letting in cool air that fanned the flames into a tempest.

The last thing Jason saw before the darkness took him was Tony's blackened body falling twitching to the floor.

CHAPTER THIRTY-TWO

"He's awake," someone yelled.

Jason moved and moaned loudly as pain flared throughout his body. He heard movement and felt something wiggle in his arm and the pain started to recede.

Other sensations slowly made their way into his consciousness. A smell of antiseptic, a slow steady beeping near his ear, a soft whooshing noise, people talking, and someone weeping off in the distance.

He tried to open his eyes. It was hard; they felt swollen. Slowly, painfully, he managed to open them a crack. A face swam before his vision. A man with dark hair and skin. "Do I know him?" he thought. Yes. Jason tried to smile but his face wouldn't work right.

"Marc?" His voice was rough and dry sounding. Like crumpled paper blowing in the wind.

The effort made him cough, wracking his beaten body with starbursts of pain all over.

"Yeah, mijo. I'm here." Jason felt a hand gently squeeze his arm.

"Where?"

"You're in Mass General."

"Why?" Jason wheezed.

"Dude, you got hurt pretty bad. Do you remember anything? The fire at work?"

Everything came flooding back: Amanda, the Acanthans, the fire. He heard the beeping getting faster and faster. Jason started to struggle. His vision went hazy, and Marc's face swam before his eyes. Marc's concerned face receded and was replaced by the face of an older woman. Deep brown skin stood out against her brightly coloured scrubs. Dark curly hair going grey at the temples and soft brown eyes that were filled with compassion.

"Shush. You're okay now. We'll take care of you," she said as she tugged at something in his arm. It stung a little when she did, but a few moments later peace washed over him, and he closed his eyes.

Jason was surrounded by columns of flame. Tony's grinning charred skull laughed at him from amidst them.

He had to get away, but he could not move. He looked down at his legs. Fire enveloped them, and Jason began to choke on the acrid smell of charring bacon.

He awoke, soaked in sweat. He was crying out and flailing in the hospital bed. Alarms screamed as monitor leads pulled away. The IV tore from his arm. Warm blood spattered his face and he screamed.

The scrubs-wearing woman was back and she'd brought friends. They held him down. He felt a jab in his arm. Slowly the panic receded, and he relaxed.

Darkness swallowed him.

This time when Jason opened his eyes it was easier.

There was less pain. Breathing wasn't easy, but it didn't hurt as much. He lay still for a moment. He moved his face. It felt less swollen. He reached up his hand to feel. His fingertips brushed cool bandages.

A warm dry hand took hold of his.

"Dude, don't. Not yet."

Jason opened his eyes. Marc was there, a stack of dog-eared books and magazines next to him on the table.

"Why?"

"You got hurt. Doc's got you bandaged up. You shouldn't poke at it."

Jason relaxed his arm and Marc laid it back down by his side, patting it gently.

"The centre?"

"CloneZone is ash, and the cops are crawling all over it." Marc grinned. "Dude, you should see it. It's all over the news. All the shit you sent out. The little bastards can't hide now."

Jason smiled back. His face felt tight.

"Amanda?"

Marc frowned and shook his head. "I'm sorry man, she's gone. She got you out, then disappeared. I haven't seen her since that night. Cops have been looking for her."

Jason sighed. "What do you mean she got me out?"

Marc smiled. "You should have seen her. She went all Batgirl on me. We got out just as the fire started. When you didn't come out, she took off back in."

Marc caught the look in Jason's eye and held up his hands. "Honest, I tried to stop her. But you didn't see her that night. She took off back into the warehouse. I thought for sure she was dead. No one could survive in there."

Marc ran his hand over his chest. "Walter managed to break two of my ribs. I was done in. We both were. I don't know how the hell she could keep going. I could barely walk."

Jason just looked at his friend and tried to shrug, flinching with the pain moving caused. Silence fell between them as they each recalled that last day at work.

Jason awoke. The scrubs woman was with him. "Morning, sunshine," she said, smiling as she helped him sit up a little. "We've met before, but you may not remember. I'm Mildred, and I'm going to be your nurse. Your surgeon, Dr. Stanford, will be in later to see you. You feeling up to it?"

Jason nodded. "Water?" he rasped.

Mildred disappeared for a minute and returned with a small plastic cup and a bendy straw.

"Easy now." She held the straw to his lips and Jason drank. The cold liquid made him choke and he coughed.

"Don't rush things. It's gonna take some time."

"How bad is it?" Jason asked after he finished coughing.

Mildred looked at him, her face serious. "I've seen worse."

"Truth."

He looked at her. She was measuring him.

"Please?"

Mildred's evaluating look changed to one of pity. It didn't make Jason feel better. "I think we should let your doctor review your injuries. You want me to stay with you?"

Jason nodded and tried to pull himself up. He couldn't feel his legs.

"Mildred…" he said, panic entering his voice.

"Oh no. Honey. Hush," she said to him, reaching down and taking his unburned hand in hers. "It's okay. It's okay." He looked up at her, terrified of what this meant.

"It's not as bad as you think. I promise. It can happen after a bad trauma."

"How? How could she think this wasn't bad?" Jason thought.

"The doctor can give you the details, but I promise you it's only temporary."

"I need to know." The nurse looked at Jason. His eyes were pleading with her. "Please?"

With a heavy sigh she sat on the edge of Jason's bed and looked him dead in the eyes.

"I'm not the one to tell you. That will be your doctor. I will promise you that we will take care of you and I'll be with you every step of the way." She stood and tucked the sheets in around Jason.

"Now rest." Mildred turned and left the room, leaving Jason with his thoughts.

As he closed his eyes, he could see Tony's laughing face before him. He wished he'd gone up with CloneZone.

EPILOGUE

Jason leaned heavily on his cane as he stared at the red brick building before him. The double glass entrance of the Maritime Museum in Halifax opened and closed as patrons entered and left, yet Jason made no move.

What awaited him there? He looked at the doors and then down at his watch; it was almost 2:30 pm. His heart began to race, but he took a deep breath, moved forward, and pushed open the doors.

Cool dry air that smelled faintly like the pages of an old book hit him and sent a shiver down his spine. He wasn't sure if it was the change in temperature or foreboding. That nagging voice of doubt crept in again, whispering, as he lined behind some tourists to wait for his turn to pay the entrance fee.

"This is crazy." He thought, "What am I doing here?"

During Jason's months in rehab, Marc had convinced him to try. Now that he was here, he was filled with anxiety and almost turned back when the young man behind the counter called out "Next."

Jason was on autopilot as he paid for his admission and held his wrist out while the clerk paused putting the paper wristband with the words "Admit 1 - Day Pass" printed on it onto Jason's arm and stared at him. He was starting to get used to the looks people would give him.

The clerk was having trouble getting the wristband on. He was trying so hard to not touch Jason's scars.

I'm sorry, sir. I don't want to hurt you." The clerk flushed with embarrassment.

Jason just smiled and finished pressing the ends of the wristband together. "Don't worry about it."

The clerk watched Jason as he walked away, wondering what he'd been through to look like that.

Without another thought, Jason headed down a carpeted corridor leading to the exhibits. His feet made soft shushing noises on the industrial carpeting while a recorded female voice provided information on the exhibits that he passed.

He followed the arrows, freezing in place before a sign that read "Titanic Exhibit – This Way." In the distance he could hear Celine Dion singing "Every night in my dreams, I see you, I feel you. That is how I know you go on." A shiver ran down his spine.

"Let me help you," she pleaded, her eyes filling with tears. "You stand a better chance with me."

He smiled down at her sadly. "No. A couple of hours ago you told me you loved me."

"I do," Amanda said. Jason could feel her hands trembling inside his own.

"Then save my friend. Get him back to his wife and kid."

"Jason…"

"Please, Amanda."

Tears threatened to slip from her eyes and her voice failed, but she nodded.

Jason snapped back to reality. That was a year ago, almost to the day. He looked at his watch again. 2:47 pm.

"I'll wait an hour," he told himself.

He knew that was a lie. He'd stay until they kicked him out. Today, tomorrow, and every day after.

A deep breath and he entered the exhibit.

A flash of blonde hair made him turn his head, his heart racing. "Amanda?" He whispered.

The person turned and Jason's face fell. It was a teen-age boy.

Wishful thinking. He walked past the heartbreaking pieces of the ship that had been salvaged, children's shoes, and ladies' gloves. Items that had torn at his heart when he was a child, but today he didn't even see them.

Every flash of blue or feminine laugh, each blonde head he saw froze him in his tracks.

He looked at his watch. 4:49 PM.

He'd been wandering for almost two hours. He felt drained. He didn't have the strength he used to, but the emotional rollercoaster of hope and failure was far worse.

Jason stopped next to a scale replica of the Titanic. He tried to lose himself in the details. It was perfect. He stared at the tiny wooden people on the deck. The tiny LED lights in the portholes. He felt the other patrons moving around him.

Someone brushed against him.

He ignored it.

A hand touched his arm, "Excuse me."

Irritated at the intrusion, Jason turned. He stopped cold when two bright blue eyes looked up at him.

"Amanda?"

ABOUT THE AUTHOR

Teresita E. Dziadura has steadily been making her voice heard in the Newfoundland writing scene more and more over the last two years, making her presence known at NaNo-WriMo writing events and seminars as a force to be reckoned with, bringing wit and insight to every conversation she's a part of.

She made her first mark in the world of published fiction with her short story 'Beyond No Man's Land' in *Chillers from the Rock*, a chilling tale that cemented her as one of the fresh new talents in the industry.

Dziadura describes herself as a sci-fi and horror nut, but is also a longtime fan of British comedy. She has studied Marine Biology and has four children with her husband of twenty-five years.

Corporate Invasion is her first novel.